The Cowboy's E-Mail Order Bride

Cora Seton

Author's Note

The Cowboy's E-Mail Order Bride is Volume 1 in the
Cowboys of Chance Creek series, set in the fictional
town of Chance Creek, Montana. To find out more
about Autumn, Ethan, Jamie, Rob, Cab and other
Chance Creek inhabitants, look for the rest of the books
in the series, including:

The Cowboy Wins a Bride (Volume 2)
The Cowboy Imports a Bride (Volume 3)
The Cowgirl Ropes a Billionaire (Volume 4)
The Sheriff Catches a Bride (Volume 5)

Visit www.coraseton.com for more titles and release
dates.

Dedication

To my husband, whose insight, love and creative spirit are always an inspiration.

Acknowledgements

I'd like to thank my family for their patience with the endless process of writing a novel, Brenda for a critique that moved things along nicely, and all the Divas for answering more questions than I can count.

Chapter One

"You did what?" Ethan Cruz turned his back on the slate and glass entrance to Chance Creek, Montana's Regional Airport, and jiggled the door handle of Rob Matheson's battered red Chevy truck. Locked. It figured - Rob had to know he'd want to turn tail and head back to town the minute he found out what his friends had done. "Open the damned door, Rob."

"Not a chance. You've got to come in – we're picking up your bride."

"I don't have a bride and no one getting off that plane concerns me. You've had your fun, now open up the door or I'm grabbing a taxi." He faced his friends. Rob, who'd lived on the ranch next door to his their entire lives. Cab Johnson, county sheriff, who was far too level-headed to be part of this mess. And Jamie Lassiter, the best horse trainer west of the Mississippi as long as you could pry him away from the ladies. The four of them had gone to school together, played football together, and spent more Saturday nights at the bar than he could count. How many times had he gotten them out of trouble, drove them home when they'd had one beer to many, listened to them bellyache about their girlfriends or lack thereof when all he really wanted to do was knock back a cold one and play a game of pool? What the hell had he ever done to deserve this?

Unfortunately, he knew exactly what he'd done. He'd played a spectacularly brilliant prank a month or so ago on Rob – a prank that still had the town buzzing – and Rob concocted this nightmare as payback. Rob got him drunk one night and egged him on about his ex-fiancee until he spilled his guts about how much it still bothered him that Lacey Taylor had given him the boot in favor of that rich sonofabitch Carl Whitfield. The name made him want to spit. Dressed like a cowboy when everyone knew he couldn't ride to save his life.

Lacey bailed on him just as life had delivered a walloping one-two punch. First his parents died in a car accident. Then he discovered the ranch was mortgaged to the hilt. As soon as Lacey learned there would be some hard times ahead, she took off like a runaway horse. Didn't even have the decency to break up with him face to face. Before he knew it Carl was flying Lacey all over creation in his private plane. Las Vegas. San Francisco. Houston. He never had a chance to get her back.

He should have kept his thoughts bottled up where they belonged – would have kept them bottled up if Rob hadn't kept putting those shots into his hand – but no, after he got done swearing and railing at Lacey's bad taste in men, he apparently decided to lecture his friends on the merits of a real woman. The kind of woman a cowboy should marry.

And Rob – good ol' Rob – captured the whole thing with his cell phone.

When he showed it to him the following day, Ethan made short work of the asinine gadget, but it was too late. Rob had already emailed the video to Cab and Jamie, and the three of them spent the next several days making his life damn miserable over it.

If only they'd left it there.

The other two would have, but Rob was still sore about that old practical joke, so he took things even further. He decided there must be a woman out there somewhere who met all of the requirements Ethan expounded on during his drunken rant. To find her, he did what any rational man would do. He edited Ethan's rant into a video advertisement for a damned mail order bride.

And posted it on YouTube.

Rob showed him the video on the ride over to the airport. There he was for all the world to see, sounding like a jack-ass – hell, looking like one, too. Rob's fancy editing made his rant sound like a proposition. "What I want," he heard himself say, "is a traditional bride. A bride for a cowboy. 18 – 25 years old, willing to work hard, beautiful, quiet, sweet, good cook, ready for children. I'm willing to give her a trial. One month'll tell me all I need to know." Then the image cut out to a screen full of text, telling women how to submit their video applications.

Unbelievable. This was low – real low – even for Rob.

Ready for children?

"You all are cracked in the head. I'm not going in there."

"Come on, Ethan," Cab said. The big man stood with his legs spread, his arms folded over his barrel chest, ready to stop him if he tried to run. "The girl's come all the way from New York. You're not even going to say hello? What kind of a fiancé are you?"

He clenched his fists. "No kind at all. And there isn't any girl in there. You know it. I know it. So stop wasting my time. There isn't any girl dumb enough to answer something like that!"

The other men exchanged a look.

"Actually," Jamie said, leaning against the Chevy and rubbing the stubble on his chin with the back of his hand. "We got nearly 200 answers to that video. Took us hours to get through them all." He grinned. "Who can resist a cowboy, right?"

As far as Ethan was concerned, plenty of women could. Lacey certainly had resisted him. Hence his bachelor status. "So you picked the ugliest, dumbest girl and tricked her into buying a plane ticket. Terrific."

Rob looked pained. "No, we found one that's both hot and smart. And we chipped in and bought the ticket – round trip, because we figured you wouldn't know a good thing when it kicked you in the butt, so we'd have to send her back. Have a little faith in your friends. You think we'd steer you wrong?"

Hell, yes. Ethan took a deep breath and squared his shoulders. The guys wouldn't admit they were joking until he'd gone into the airport and hung around the gate looking foolish for a suitable amount of time. And if they were stupid enough to actually fly a girl out here, he couldn't trust them to put her back on a plane home. So now instead of finishing his chores before supper, he'd lose the rest of the afternoon sorting out this mess.

"Fine. Let's get this over with," he said, striding toward the front door. Inside, he didn't bother to look at the television screen which showed incoming and outgoing flights. Chance Creek Regional had all of four gates. He'd just follow the hall as far as homeland security allowed him and wait until some lost soul deplaned.

"Look – it's on time." Rob grabbed his arm and tried to hurry him along. Ethan dug in the heels of his well worn boots and proceeded at his own pace.

Jamie pulled a cardboard sign out from under his jacket and flashed it at Ethan before holding it up above his head. It read, *Autumn Leeds*. Jamie shrugged at Ethan's expression. "I know – the name's brutal."

"Want to see her?" Cab pulled out a gadget and handed it over. Ethan held it gingerly. The laptop he bought on the advice of his accountant still sat untouched in his tiny office back at the ranch. He hated these miniature things that ran on swoops and swipes and taps on buttons that weren't really there. Cab reached over and pressed something and it came to life, showing a pretty young woman in a cotton dress in a kitchen preparing what appeared to be a pot roast.

"Hi, I'm Autumn," she said, looking straight at him. "Autumn Leeds. As you can see, I love cooking…"

Rob whooped and pointed. "Look – there she is! I told you she'd come!"

Ethan raised his gaze from the gadget to see the woman herself walking toward them down the carpeted hall. Long black hair, startling blue eyes, porcelain-white skin, she was thin and haunted and luminous all at the same time. She, too, held a cell phone and seemed to be consulting it, her gaze glancing down then sweeping the crowd. As their eyes met, hers widened with recognition. He groaned inwardly when he realized this pretty woman had probably watched Rob's stupid video multiple times. She might be looking at his picture now.

As the crowd of passengers and relatives split around their party, she walked straight up to them and held out her hand. "Ethan Cruz?" Her voice was low and husky, her fingers cool and her handshake firm. He found himself wanting to linger over it. Instead he nodded. "I'm Autumn Leeds. Your bride."

Autumn had never been more terrified in her life. In her short career as a columnist for CityPretty Magazine, she'd interviewed models, society women, CEO's and politicians, but all of them were urbanites, and she'd never had to leave New York to get the job done. As soon as her plane departed LaGuardia she knew she'd made a mistake. As the city skyline fell away and the countryside below her emptied into farmland, she clutched the arms of her seat as if she was heading for the moon rather than Montana. Now, hours later, she felt off-kilter and fuzzy, and the four men before her looked like extras in a Western flick. Large, muscled, rough men who all exuded a distinct odor of sweat she realized probably came from an honest afternoon's work. Entirely out of her comfort zone, she wondered for the millionth time if she'd done the right thing. *It's the only way to get my contract renewed*, she reminded herself. She had to write a story different from all the other articles in CityPretty. In these tough economic times, the magazine was downsizing – again. If she didn't want to find herself out on the street, she had to produce – fast.

And what better story to write than the tale of a Montana cowboy using YouTube to search for an email-order bride?

Ethan Cruz looked back at her, seemingly at a loss for words. Well, that was to be expected with a cowboy, right? The ones in movies said about one word every ten minutes or so. That's why his video said she needed to be quiet. Well, she could be quiet. She didn't trust herself to speak, anyway.

She'd never been so near a cowboy before. Her best friend, Becka, helped shoot her video response, and they'd spent a hilarious day creating a pseudo-Autumn guaranteed to warm the cockles of a cowboy's heart. Together, they'd decided to pitch her as desperate to escape the dirty city and unleash her inner farm wife on Ethan's Montana ranch. They hinted she loved gardening, canning, and all the domestic arts. They played up both her toughness (she played first base in high school baseball) and her femininity (she loved quilting – *what an outright lie*). She had six costume changes in the three minute video.

Over her vehement protests, Becka forced her to end the video with a close-up of her face while she uttered the words, "I often fall asleep imagining the family I'll someday have." Autumn's cheeks warmed as she recalled the depth of the deception. She wasn't a country girl pining to be a wife; she was a career girl who didn't intend to have kids for at least another decade. Right?

Of course.

Except somehow, when she watched the final video, the life the false Autumn said she wanted sounded far more compelling than the life the real Autumn lived. Especially the part about wanting a family.

It wasn't that she didn't want a career. She just wanted a different one – a different life. She hated how hectic and shallow everything seemed now. She remembered her childhood, back when she had two parents - a successful investment banker father and a stay-at-home mother who made the best cookies in New York City. Back then, her mom, Teresa, loved to take Autumn and her sister, Lily, to visit museums, see movies and plays, walk in Central Park and shop in the ethnic groceries that surrounded their home. On Sundays, they cooked fabulous feasts together and her mother's laugh rang out loud and often. Friends and relatives stopped by to eat and talk, and Autumn played with the other children while the grownups clustered around the kitchen table. All that changed when she turned nine and her father left them for a travel agent. Her parents' divorce was horrible. The fight wasn't over custody; her father was all too eager to leave child-rearing to her mother while he toured Brazil with his new wife. The fight was over money – over the bulk of the savings her father had transferred to offshore accounts in the weeks before the breakup, and refused to return.

Broke, single and humiliated, her mother took up the threads of the life she'd put aside to marry and raise a family. A graduate of an elite liberal arts college, with several years of medical school already under her belt, she moved them into a tiny apartment on the edge of a barely-decent neighborhood and returned to her studies. Those were lean, lonely years when everyone had to pitch in. Autumn's older sister watched over her after school, and Teresa expected them to take on any and all chores they could possibly handle. As Autumn grew, she took over the cooking and shopping and finally the family's accounts. Teresa had no time for cultural excursions, let alone entertaining friends, but by the time Autumn was ready to go to college herself, she ran a successful OB-GYN practice that catered to wealthy women who'd left childbearing until the last possible moment, and she didn't even have to take out a loan to fund her education.

Determined her daughters would never face the same challenges she had, Teresa raised them with three guiding precepts:

Every woman must be self-supporting.

Marriage is a trap set by men for women.

Parenthood must be postponed until one reaches the pinnacle of her career.

Autumn's sister, Lily, was a shining example of this guide to life. She was single, ran her own physical therapy clinic, and didn't plan to marry or have children any time soon. Next to her, Autumn felt like a black sheep. She couldn't seem to accept work was all there was to life. Couldn't forget the joy of laying a table for a host of guests. She still missed those happy, crowded Sunday afternoons so much it hurt her to think about them.

She forced her thoughts back to the present. The man before her was ten times more handsome than he was in his video, and that was saying a lot. Dark hair, blue eyes, a chiseled jaw with just a trace of manly stubble. His shoulders were broad and his stance radiated a determination she found more than compelling. This was a man you could lean on, a man who could take care of the bad guys, wrangle the cattle, and still sweep you off your feet.

"Ethan, aren't you going to say hello to your fiancée?" One of the other men stuck out his hand.

"I'm Rob Matheson. This is Cab Johnson and Jamie Lassiter. Ethan here needed some backup."

Rob was blonde, about Ethan's size, but not nearly so serious. In fact, she bet he was a real cut-up. That shit-eating grin probably never left his face. Cab was larger than the others – six foot four maybe, powerfully built. He wore a sheriff's uniform. Jamie was lean but muscular, with dark brown hair that fell into his eyes. They had the easy camaraderie that spoke of a long acquaintance. They probably knew each other as kids, and would take turns being best man at each other's weddings.

Her wedding.

No – she'd be long gone before the month was up. She had three weeks to turn in the story; maybe four, if it was really juicy. She'd pitched it to the editor of CityPretty as soon as the idea occurred to her. Margaret's uncertain approval told her she was probably allowing her one last hurrah before CityPretty let her go.

Still, just for one moment she imagined herself standing side by side Ethan at the altar of some country church, pledging her love to him. What would it be like to marry a near stranger and try to forge a life with him?

Insane, that's what.

So why did the idea send tendrils of warmth into all the right places?

She glanced up at Ethan to find him glancing down, and the warm feeling curved around her insides again. Surely New York men couldn't be shorter than this crew, or any less manly, but she couldn't remember the last time she'd been around so much blatant testosterone. She must be ovulating. Why else would she react like this to a perfect stranger?

Ethan touched her arm. "This way." She followed him down the hall, the others falling into place behind them like a cowboy entourage. She stifled a sudden laugh at the absurdity of it all, slipped her hand into her purse and grabbed her digital camera, capturing the scene with a few clicks. Had this man – this...cowboy – sat down and planned out the video he'd made? She tried to picture Ethan bending over a desk and carefully writing out "Sweet. Good cook. *Ready for children.*"

She blew out a breath and wondered if she was the only one stifling in this sudden heat. Ready for children? Hardly. Still...if she was going to make babies with anyone...

Shaking her head to dispel that dangerous image, she found herself at the airport's single baggage carousel. It was just shuddering to life and within moments she pointed out first one, then another sleek, black suitcase. Ethan took them both, began to move toward the door and then faltered to a stop. He avoided her gaze, focusing on something far beyond her shoulder. "It's just...I wasn't...."

Oh God, Autumn thought, a sudden chill racing down her spine. Her stomach lurched and she raised a hand as if to ward off his words. She hadn't even considered this.

He'd taken one look and decided to send her back.

Ethan stared into the stricken eyes of the most beautiful woman he'd ever met. He had to confess to her right now the extent of the joke she'd been led into thinking was real. It'd been bad enough when he thought Rob and the rest of them had simply hauled him to the airport for a chance to laugh their asses off at him, but now there was a woman involved, a real, beautiful, fragile woman. He had to stop this before it went any further.

When she raised her clear blue gaze to his, he saw panic, horror, and an awful recognition he instantly realized meant she thought she'd been judged and found wanting. He knew he'd do anything to make that look go away. Judged wanting. As if. The girl was as beautiful as a harvest moon shining on frost-flecked fields in late November. He itched to touch her, take her hand, pull her hard against him and...

Whoa – that thought couldn't go any farther.

He swallowed hard and tried again. "I...it's just my place...something came up and I didn't get a chance to fix it like I meant to." She relaxed a fraction and he rushed on. "It's a good house – built by my great granddaddy in 1889 for the hired help. Solid. Just needs a little attention."

"A woman's touch," Rob threw in.

Ethan restrained himself, barely. He'd get back at all of his friends soon enough. "I just hope you'll be comfortable."

A snigger behind him made him clench his fists.

"I don't mind if it's rough," Autumn said, eliciting a bark of laughter from the peanut gallery. She blushed and Ethan couldn't take his eyes off her face, although he wished she hadn't caught the joke. She'd look like that in bed, after…

Enough.

"Give me the keys," he said to Rob. When his friend hesitated, he held out a hand. "Now."

Rob handed them over with a raised eyebrow, but Ethan just led the way outside and threw Autumn's suitcases in the bed of the truck. He opened the passenger side door.

"Thank you," she said, putting first one foot, then the other on the running board and scrambling somewhat ungracefully into the seat. City girl. At least her hesitation gave him a long moment to enjoy the view.

Rob made as if to open the door to the back bench seat, but Ethan shoved him aside, pressed down the lock and closed the passenger door. He was halfway around the truck before Rob could react.

"Hey, what are you doing?"

"Taking a ride with my fiancée. You all find your own way home." He was in the driver's side with the ignition turning over before any of them moved a muscle. Stupid fools. They'd made their beds and they could sleep in them.

He glanced at the ethereal princess sitting less than two feet away. Meanwhile, he'd sleep in his own comfortable bed tonight. Maybe with a little company for once.

Chapter Two

Fatigue overtook her as soon as they gained the highway. Autumn hadn't slept a wink the night before, excitement over the challenge of the undercover assignment, something she hadn't attempted before, alternating with fear of exposure, or worse – failure. She didn't know what to expect, or how far she could string this man along before she had to admit it was all a ruse.

Actually, she hoped she'd never have to admit to her deception. She and Becka had carefully concocted an escape story – a dead aunt whose funeral Autumn had to attend. If things got too rough, she'd whip out her excuse and be on the next plane to New York. Then she'd write her story and Ethan would never even know about it. Montana cowboys didn't read CityPretty, did they?

She wondered if she could spin the article off into something longer. Maybe give it a "where is our culture going" edge and send it in to New Yorker magazine? Or play up the romantic aspect and sell it to Cosmo?

Perhaps she could write a book?

"You hungry?"

Autumn jumped. She'd all but forgotten the man driving the pickup. "Sorry?"

"Are you hungry? We could grab a burger." He pointed at a mom and pop joint coming up on the right. She arched an eyebrow. Really? His first meal with his fiancée and the cowboy was going to take her to a burger joint? She bit back a smile. This article was going to write itself.

He seemed to realize his mistake. "Or, we could grab a steak at DelMonaco's Grill."

"Sure. That sounds nice."

Darn, CityPretty's readers loved snarky articles that skewered the mannerisms of the lesser orders – that is, anyone who wasn't a young, upwardly mobile urbanite. If she could portray Ethan and his friends as a bunch of country bumpkins, so much the better. She frowned, as uncomfortable with this type of journalism as she had been her first day on the job. What could she do, though? She needed to eat.

Ethan accelerated and she watched the burger joint slip past into the rear view mirror. The silence between them lengthened until she clutched the floral print fabric of her dress with both hands to try to keep from talking. She wasn't accustomed to long silences. New Yorkers talked a mile a minute; especially her co-workers.

"Did you grow up around here?" she asked several minutes later when she couldn't stand it anymore.

"Yep. I live on the same ranch where I was born."

"Oh – is your family still there, too?" She'd never thought about that and she experienced a moment of real fear. She could fool a young cowboy…maybe. But a cowboy's mama? That sounded a lot harder.

"My folks are gone. Died in an accident last year."

"I'm sorry." And she was. Really. But relieved, too. How sick was that?

"Got a sister in Billings. I see her now and then."

She nodded, fascinated by the muscle that tightened along the line of his jaw. There was a story there, she was sure of it. What did his sister do that made him so tense? And how did he make every plain Jane sentence he uttered sound so damn sexy? He was talking about his family, but he could have been crooning a love song with that rough, masculine tone. Maybe she should have crossed the Mississippi a long time ago.

Hormones. Ovulating. Get a grip, Autumn.

"What about you?" he asked, glancing her way for a fraction of a second. "Your folks still alive?"

"Yes. My mom lives in Manhattan. Dad's long gone. Last I heard he was in Rio."

"You grew up in the city, but you hate it?"

"No, I…" She let the sentence trail off. Whoops, nearly blew her cover story already. "Right," she said with a forced smile. "I hate it. I can't wait to get out of there for good."

He gave her a measured look. "Isn't that why you're here?"

"Right!" she said again. "Yeah. I just…I mean…maybe you and I…" Man, she had to pull herself together, fast, or he'd see through her in a minute. "I mean, I hope it works out – you know, between you and me."

She couldn't look at him, and she noticed he was keeping his eyes on the road now. "Yeah. Me, too," he said gruffly. "Here we are."

What the hell was he saying? Ethan pulled sharply into a parking spot and hit the brakes, grinding the Chevy to a stop. This was insane. He had to tell her she'd been fooled before the whole thing got out of hand. Oh, who was he kidding; the situation was already far past out of hand. He took a deep breath and considered his next move. The least he could do was buy the pretty lady next to him a nice steak dinner before he broke the news. That way he could ask her a few more questions – find out why a woman like her would ditch her job and family back in New York and fly all the way out here to get married to a perfect stranger.

Who did that kind of thing, anyway?

He looked her over out of the corner of his eye as he slid his seatbelt off and exited the truck. Walking around the cab, he opened her door and tried not to stare at the expanse of her leg visible as she slid out of the seat. She smoothed her dress down as soon as she hit the pavement, but not before he got a pretty clear view of her shapely thighs.

Come on, Ethan, you've seen lots of legs before.

But none that affected him quite like this. Not even Lacey's.

He had to admit part of it was knowing this woman had voluntarily come all the way from New York to marry him. *Him.* Based solely on the asinine video Rob put up on the web, she'd deemed him worthy of being her partner, protector – and lover – for the rest of her life. The prettiest package he'd ever seen and she'd delivered herself right to his door – practically.

What if he didn't tell her it was a joke? What if he just married her?

The idea was more promising than he ever could have imagined a half hour ago. He followed her up the walkway to DelMonaco's, appreciating the way her thin cotton dress conformed to the curves of her body. She didn't look like a city girl in that outfit. She looked womanly, soft, at home in the country – but maybe that was the point. She was selling herself to him, in a way.

DelMonaco's was hopping, as it always was on Saturday nights, but they were lucky and got a table after only a minute or two of waiting. Sarah-Jane, the hostess, who he'd gone to high school with, led them to a small, square table in the middle of the restaurant. Ethan saw her give Autumn more than one appraising look, but she didn't ask any questions and he was grateful for that. He pulled out a wooden chair for her, and took the one kitty-corner to it.

"The food must be good here," Autumn said, looking over the menu.

"There aren't that many places to go." Ethan scanned his menu as well, although he knew it by heart. He ordered the same thing every time he came. Porter house steak, baked potato, coleslaw. None of that salad bar stuff for him.

"Well, look who's here!"

Ethan stiffened, his fingers crumpling the laminated menu. A week ago he would have given anything to hear that voice, but not now. Definitely not now.

He forced himself to loosen his grip on the menu and look up at the couple who'd stopped next to his table. Lacey Taylor, dressed in a skimpy sundress that barely grazed the tops of her thighs, strappy white sandals, and a diamond on her finger you could use to signal Mars, smiled down at him. Behind her stood Carl Whitfield, in denim jeans, cowboy boots, a blazer and a string tie. Reflexively, a slow burn started in Ethan's stomach. Everything about Lacey's new boyfriend made him want to punch the man's lights out. He'd come to Chance Creek looking for a ranch to buy, and took his time ferreting out the most desperate rancher so he could cut a bargain that would make the devil applaud. Someone would be coming after Ethan's ranch like that pretty soon, but he'd be damned if he'd sell.

Lacey's smile widened as if she'd read his thoughts. "Hi Ethan! We're celebrating our eight month anniversary. Can you believe we've been dating that long? Only six months to the wedding! I can't wait until Carl makes an honest woman of me."

Had Lacey's smile always been so fake? And since when did she wear all that makeup? Suddenly Ethan couldn't see why he'd always thought she was so attractive. Sure, she had curves in all the right places and her platinum blonde hair could dazzle a man, but next to Autumn she seemed so...plastic.

"We're going on the Grand Tour for our honeymoon," Carl said, reaching forward to shake Ethan's hand. "France, Italy, Greece, Austria..."

"Carl says we'll just keep going until we get so homesick we have to come back," Lacey gushed. "Can you imagine ever getting sick for this little town? I told him we'll be gone forever!"

"Can't stay away forever, darling," Carl said. "You have to decorate that mansion I've been building just for you."

"I get to pick out all the furniture!" she practically squealed. "Can you believe it?"

When Ethan didn't answer, her smile faded a notch and she turned her gaze to Autumn. "Oh, hi," she said. "I'm Lacey. Ethan's probably told you about me."

Autumn shrugged and Ethan fought down the urge to kiss her. Nothing irked Lacey more than not being the center of attention – another fact about her that seemed much clearer than it had just 24 hours ago.

"Sorry, he didn't mention you. Are you his sister?"

Ethan bit back a laugh at the look on Lacey's face. Autumn definitely earned a kiss for that.

"Sister?" Lacey was outraged. "No. I'm his...was...his fiancée. Who are you?"

Autumn glanced at him. "Oh, I'm...Autumn. I'm Ethan's..."

"His new fiancée!" Suddenly Rob was there behind him, trailed by Cab and Jamie. He put a hand on Ethan's shoulder and gave it a not so friendly squeeze. "They're getting married. Isn't that sweet!"

"Rob!" Ethan growled. His friend let him go and tousled his hair.

"Sorry, I know it's supposed to be a secret, but I can't help myself. I spent thirty dollars on a cab ride just now so I could be here and share your joy." Damn, he should have realized when he left Rob stranded at the airport he'd only added fuel to the fire of his need for revenge.

The practical joke he'd played on Rob last month was a good one, but Rob was doing a damn fine job of getting back at him. In fact, he'd say they were quits right about now.

Lacey's mouth opened, but no sound came out. After a long moment, Carl said, "Congratulations! Well, hey now – marriages are bursting out all over the place, aren't they!"

Lacey looked like she wanted to slug him. "You never said you were dating again, Ethan. When did you two meet?"

"Today," Autumn answered at the same time he said, "A few years ago."

Lacey looked from one to the other. "Uh uh, I smell a fake. You're putting me on, Ethan Cruz. You're just pretending to be engaged because you're jealous of me and Carl."

The anger that had simmered in his gut for the past eight months since she'd dumped him burst into flame. "Lacey, the last thing I am is jealous of you and Carl. I have Autumn, and I'm making her my wife. Next month. June 21st."   Before anyone could say a thing, he leaned over the corner of the table, cupped Autumn's head, pulled her close, and gave her a kiss so smoldering it put a prairie fire to shame.

When Ethan released her, Autumn gasped for air, raising a hand to her lips. No one had ever kissed her like that – not even the man she'd lived with for nearly a year when she was twenty. For a moment her head spun and she couldn't make out what the others were saying, but while Lacey looked furious, her fiancé – Carl, was it? – looked like he'd just taken the prize at a turkey shoot. He raised his hands above his head and clapped them together. The noisy restaurant crowd hushed, craning their necks to see what was happening in the center of the room.

"Folks! Folks, can I have your attention for a moment?" Carl called. "I've got great news! Our own hometown boy, Ethan Cruz, has caught himself a fiancée! What's your name, honey?" He bent down toward her.

"Um...Autumn," she said.

"Autumn! That's her name. Let's give a round of applause for the happy couple! May they have a long and happy marriage! Barkeep!" Autumn cringed – did people really say that here? "A round of champagne for the house – on me!"

Applause split the air as Carl thumped Ethan on the back. Then he made them stand up while the rowdy Saturday night crowd cheered. "Kiss! Kiss!" he crowed and the rest of the patrons soon joined in. Autumn wanted to sink into the floor. What had happened to keeping a low profile and slipping away before the month was out? Looking up at Ethan she saw the same glazed look in his eyes she was sure was in her own. He dutifully bent down and kissed her again.

She meant to keep it short and sweet and she was sure he did, too, but the moment their lips met electricity sparked between them and she found didn't want to move away. His hand slid around her waist and soon she was pressed against him, tilting her head up and standing on tip-toe to meet his embrace. Her skin tingled every place she touched him, a heat building up inside her that had long been absent in her life. When he slid his hand down her back, she leaned into him, too far gone in their kiss to care that everyone in the room was watching them.

"Hey, save something for the honeymoon!" Carl laughed. They broke apart and Autumn, breathless, noticed the furious expression on Lacey's face. Poor girl. Probably just realizing the catch she'd let slip her hook. Carl cupped his fiancee's elbow and moved her away, calling back a few last congratulations. The crowd settled down for the moment and she took the chance to sit again. She went back to studying the menu, although when Sarah-Jane returned to take their orders, she still hadn't made a choice.

"Something light?" she said in desperation. For some reason she couldn't focus on the menu's printed words. The names of the specials danced in front of her as she relived, time and time again, the feel of Ethan's mouth on hers, the way his hands caressed her, and the passion that had flared to life within her at his briefest touch. It must be the plane ride or the time change – or her hormones – that made her so sensitive. She wasn't accustomed to falling hard for strangers.

Sarah-Jane saved her. "I'll bring an order of Chicken Tuscany and you can make your way to the salad bar whenever you're ready."

"Thanks." She waited until Ethan ordered his steak and Sarah-Jane carted off the menus, then rose again. "I'll be back in a minute."

Ethan stood up, too, and helped pull back her chair. A gentleman. She liked that. "I'll be waiting."

His laconic sentence and the way his gaze lingered on hers brought another rush of heat to her cheeks. Waiting…for what? For her return, or for something else entirely? Had he felt some kind of connection, too? Was he looking forward to later tonight, when they were alone?

She hurried off and found the ladies room, refusing to make eye contact with any of the other patrons trying to get her attention and give her their congratulations. Locking herself into a stall she took a minute to sort out everything that had just happened. Ethan obviously took this marriage thing very seriously. Somehow she thought they'd spend some time together before he brought up the actual engagement, although now that seemed naïve. The man wanted a wife and he wanted one right now. Why else put a video like that up on YouTube.

I can't do this. I have to leave tonight.

But even as she thought it she knew it was a lie. She'd do anything to get this story and clinch her contract with CityPretty. Writing for a magazine was the one goal she'd ever reached in life and she wasn't going to lose that achievement now, just because a cowboy's kisses sent her around the bend.

I'll see this through until the end.

She wouldn't give her mother or sister another reason to call her a failure. Bad enough she hadn't gone into medicine like they did. Bad enough she'd ever mentioned going to culinary school. Bad enough when she'd *listened to reason* and gone to a university instead, she'd switched from pre-med to majoring in English. Bad enough she'd bailed from the internship her mother had set up for her to travel to England with Becka instead. Bad enough she'd refused to get her Masters and PhD so she could be a professor.

Bad enough she was a writer. A writer for a women's magazine.

If she lost her job now it would mean one more family chorus of "I told you so," and another disappointment for them to chalk up on their score cards. She could not bear that. So she would see this assignment through to the bitter end, no matter what it took.

As she flushed the toilet and made her way to the sinks, she didn't allow herself to think about just what that might mean.

Ethan watched Autumn snake her way back through the tables, stopping every few feet to shake hands and receive congratulations from well-wishers among the diners. As she chatted with a few, he caught a look of naked worry on her face and realized she was out of her depth making up details of their relationship on the fly. They'd better put their heads together and sync up their stories tonight before one of them slipped up.

When she reached their table, she glanced at the extra chairs, now filled with Rob, Cab and Jamie, who were happily destroying the contents of a bread basket and quenching their thirst with a pitcher of beer. She slipped into the seat next to him and whispered in his ear. "I've been telling everyone you'd fill them in on how we met. I didn't know what you wanted me to say. Don't they know about your video?"

"No," Ethan hissed. "Well, except for these guys. And I'd like to keep it that way. It's embarrassing," he added when she gave him a questioning look. "I didn't think many people would see it."

"You put a video on YouTube and thought no one would look at it?"

Damn. He thought fast. "Just follow my lead. We've known each other off and on for a couple years. After Lacey bailed, I got back in touch. We've had a long distance relationship for the past six months."

She nodded. "Okay. How about, we couldn't stand being apart any longer but I'm a traditionalist; no living together until there's a ring on my finger. We'll say I'm a bit of a control freak and wouldn't let you pick it alone."

A ring.

"How much is that gonna cost me?" The words were out before he thought them through and she rewarded him with a look that seemed half-disgust, half-hurt. Shit. He kept forgetting she was here because she believed this was for real – she wasn't in on the joke. A joke that had gone way too far. He wiped his hands on his jeans under the table and gathered his courage. He hated to do it like this – in public, especially after the upwelling of support from the community they'd just witnessed, but better to do it now – to pull the band-aid off quickly, so to speak – than to wait for things to get even worse.

"Look, Autumn," he began, leaning toward her.

"I guess…I always wanted something simple," she said, the hurt still there in her voice. "I don't need a fancy ring to prove that I believe in always and forever."

The words he meant to say vanished.

Always and forever.

Was she for real? After all the blows he'd been dealt this past year, was fate finally turning on its head and offering him a gift? Always and forever was exactly what he wanted. Well, what he used to want – until his mother and Lacey showed him how little a woman's vows meant.

"We'll find something pretty," he heard himself say. "Something pretty for a pretty girl."

She blushed. The sweet, curvy, beautiful woman sitting next to him actually blushed. He couldn't help himself. He leaned in and kissed her on the cheek. Straightening up, he caught Rob's knowing smile, but before he could think of something biting to say to wipe it off, Sarah-Jane came to the table with two more pitchers of beer.

"On the house – from the Winters." She nodded to a couple smiling and waving from across the room. Dave Winters was Ethan's 10th grade shop class teacher. He forced himself to smile and raise a glass in appreciation. Damn it, what was he thinking kissing

Autumn? Promising her a ring! Had he gone completely insane?

"Drink up!" Cab shouted. "And kiss the girl! Kiss! Kiss! Kiss!" In a moment the whole crowd was chanting along.

Not again.

Autumn raised her glass to his, then drank deeply. He followed suit, not knowing what else to do. For tonight, they were caught like deer in the headlights of this crowd's enthusiasm. Rob had won for now. He'd drink. He'd kiss the girl. Tomorrow, however, he would sort this out once and for all, put Autumn on a plane back to New York City and give Rob the whupping of his life for hurting the most desirable woman he'd ever met.

He downed his drink, slipped a hand under Autumn's silky hair and pulled her close, then kissed the daylights out of her. The crowd went wild.

It was a tight fit in Rob's truck at the end of the night since Jamie picked up some female company. Autumn didn't care. She didn't care about anything. She'd drunk more beer than she thought humanly possible, been kissed more times in one night than she'd been in three years. She'd lost wildly at pool and darts in DelMonaco's games room, danced with more cowboys than she could count on DelMonaco's poor excuse for a dance floor while being serenaded by its juke box, and taken pictures of everything.

She was dizzy, sleepy, and warm all over from the excess of human contact she'd experienced. Now she perched on Ethan's lap, one arm around his neck, because it was the only way they fit in the back seat of the extended cab, crammed in next to Jamie and Sheila somebody – a loud talking cowgirl all the men seemed to know. Ethan's arms circled her waist and one hand rested on her thigh. The heat of it was sending shivers of desire up and down her body. How long had it been since she had been held and caressed? Ethan's battered jacket covered her since the night had turned cool. She snuggled under it, her face pressed to his neck. He smelled so good – so different from men in New York. Not a whiff of cologne on him. She realized in a rush what a turn-off it was that so many of the men in New York used more product than she did.

Ethan used good old soap and shampoo, she'd bet. She pressed her nose further into his skin and breathed in long and hard. Yummy. Did he taste as good as he smelled? She pressed her lips against his neck and allowed her tongue to dart out. Yep. Delicious. She tried it again.

Ethan stiffened, then tightened his hold on her, his hand on her thigh smoothing down her skirt, then traveling to her waist, then higher still. When it brushed against her breast, her breath caught and she stilled, waiting for that caress to go on. After a moment so long it felt like a lifetime, it did. His hand curved around the swell of her breast and lightly squeezed. A rush of heat warmed her and she leaned into him, biting her lip when his fingers found her nipple and began to tease it through the fabric of her bra and dress.

She kissed him harder, straining to reach his ear, down his neck, under his chin. His touch grew stronger, surer, the sweep of his hand around her breast setting her on fire and the pass of his thumb over her increasingly sensitive nipple nearly driving her to moan out loud.

"Okay, you two – get a room!" Rob called over the seat.

Autumn pulled away from Ethan with a gasp and met Rob's gaze in the rear view mirror. The cowboy's mocking grin made her turn away and look out of the truck. They'd stopped in a driveway before a long, low house. A single lightbulb on the porch broke the darkness that seemed to spread for miles in every direction. This must be Ethan's ranch. She shivered at the sudden realization they were alone out here. Well, alone with four rowdy cowboy friends.

Cab got out of the front seat and opened the door for them. Ethan scooped her into his arms and slid out of the truck, landing hard but keeping his footing in the dirt of the driveway. Not acknowledging the whoops and cheers from his friends, he walked toward the front door of the small structure before them, carrying her as if it was something he did daily. She heard the truck turn in the driveway with a roar of its engines. He stumped up the steps, fumbled with the doorknob for a moment, then carried her indoors and slammed the door shut behind them.

She saw an unembellished living room, neat but spare, a door leading into a kitchen she only glimpsed, a flash of hall, and then they were in a bedroom. A man's bedroom. Dark colors. Solid furniture. He set her gently on her feet and bent to turn on the bedside lamp. He threw the comforter back on the large bed.

"If you want out, now's the time to say so," he said, his breath tickling her chin.

Warning bells clanged in her mind, but Autumn pushed them back. The last thing she wanted was out. She kissed him full on the mouth, hard.

"I'm in."

This had to be a dream, Ethan thought. Things like this didn't happen to guys like him. When Lacey ditched him he swore he'd never be fooled by a woman again, and here he was with a dream girl, hand delivered to him, ready, willing and able not just to share his bed, but his life.

Forever and always. Her exact words. Hell yeah he'd buy her a ring. He'd put the biggest diamond he could afford on her finger and then together they'd save this ranch of his. They would undo everything his mother had done, pay back the bank, silence his creditors, buy out his sister, and show everyone that the Cruz's might be down and out, but they weren't finished. Far from it.

As Autumn sat down on the bed he shucked off his shirt and undid the buckle of his jeans. Pure lust raged through his body and he couldn't stand the distance between them for one more minute. Judging from the look in her eyes, neither could she.

She began to work on the buttons that did up the back of her dress. He kicked off his boots and jeans, turned her around and swept her hair aside. The buttons were small and difficult for his large fingers, but he made short work of them. Shucking off his boxers, he turned her once more gently around and waited for her to do the rest.

Her eyes widened at the sight of him, naked and ready, and a wicked smile played on her lips as she looked him up and down. "You are something," she said.

"Hurry up."

She laughed, and the sound fueled his desire.

"Need some help?"

"I got it." She slid the dress first off one shoulder, then the other, then down to her waist. She unhooked her lacy bra, and let that fall, too. Ethan couldn't wait a moment more. He swept down, took one nipple into his mouth and tipped her over, pulling her into his arms.

Alone at last, their audience long gone, Autumn chucked all propriety to the wind. In for a penny, in for a pound. She was going to enjoy this night with this helluva man and damn the consequences. As he lay her down, the world spun around her and she knew she'd drunk far too much. She wasn't thinking clearly. His mouth on her skin was doing delicious things to her insides, coiling them up into golden ropes of desire. He couldn't kiss enough of her, couldn't suck hard enough on her nipples, couldn't touch enough of her at once.

She writhed in his arms as he moved from one breast to the other, playing with them, loving them, nipping and laving and teasing her until she wanted to scream from delighted agony. Then he moved lower, kissing her belly, her mound, and then....Oh, God... she clutched the sheets. Oh God, that felt good. She coiled her fingers in his hair, let him drive her to the edge of oblivion, and groaned when he pulled back.

"Ethan," she cried, and he was there, the length of his body pressed against hers, one hand cradling her head, the other pulling her tight. "I can't wait," she breathed. "Now!" Something tugged at her consciousness – a little voice telling her she was forgetting something. Birth control. Shouldn't she...?

And he was in her, one thrust taking him all the way home. She gasped aloud, then cried out in sheer pleasure. He smiled, a predatory, knowing grin, pulled out and stroked in again. She didn't hold back, her moan filling the room, letting him know just how much she wanted him. She slid her hands to his ass, gripped him tight and pulled him against her. He got the message.

Their lovemaking was like nothing she'd ever known. Fast, hard, passionate, each of them wanting, needing more. He filled her and moved her and slammed into her until the heat and pressure between her thighs built to a peak of tension she couldn't resist.

"Ethan!"

He pushed into her a final time with his own cry of triumph and they came together with an intensity that shocked Autumn to the roots of her soul. Wave after wave of heat and light consumed her body, and she cried out again and again. When it was over she lay back, spent, Ethan sprawled on top of her. She welcomed his weight, welcomed the touch of his lips on her eyelids, nose, cheeks and mouth. And as she drifted off to sleep, she smiled contentedly, knowing that tomorrow they would do this again.

Chapter Three

What had he done?

Ethan stood on the front porch of the bunkhouse he'd converted into his home, and gazed across the yard at the big house he'd grown up in, letting the cool morning air blow over his shirtless torso. He gripped a cup of coffee in one hand like it was a lifeline, and in a way it was. His head ached, his mind refused to think clearly. All he knew was that in the 24 hours since he'd watched his last sunrise over the fields of his family's ranch from this very same spot, he'd acquired a fiancée, lied to just about everyone he knew about his intentions toward her, and had the most riveting sexual experience of his life.

With a stranger.

A stranger he intended to put on a plane and send away this very morning.

The acid burning in his belly and the back of his throat wasn't due to the copious amounts of alcohol he'd consumed the night before. It was the product of the knowledge that before sundown the whole damn town would be sneering at him. Ethan the cheat. Ethan the loser. Ethan, the man who lures defenseless women to town for a quick roll in the hay, then sends them packing. Ethan, who can't even hold onto the ranch that'd been in his family for generations.

No matter that Rob was the joker who had set this whole fiancée thing in motion. No matter that Lacey made him a loser in the love department. No matter that his own mother had siphoned off the ranch's earnings for years to support her outrageous spending sprees.

In the end it all came down to him. His inability to control his world. His inability to right the wrongs of others. No one else could be trusted to make things right. He had to do it all, or die trying.

His knuckles stood out white against the mug and he forced himself to relax his grip. He'd been through some tough times before and this one wouldn't kill him, either. He thought his parents' deaths would be the end of him; two of the people he loved most in the world snuffed out with no chance to say good-bye. He remembered the night the state troopers knocked on his door, broke the news man to man, then left him to the realization that he was all alone. He barely had time to absorb the shock before all the responsibilities of running a ranch came crashing down on his shoulders. Cattle, horses, men, all depending on him to keep things right.

He'd reached out to his sister then, but she'd turned him down flat. Claire had left for Billings years ago to become an interior designer after a particularly nasty argument with their mother. No way she was coming home to help, not even for a couple of weeks. She offered to find a realtor to list the spread and he'd hung up on her. It was months before they spoke again.

Then came another shock – the day he spent with his parents' accountant, going over the books for the Cruz spread for the first time. He had no idea how much money his mother spent on her annual jaunts to Europe. No idea how thin the ranch's margin was. His parents were in debt up to their eyeballs when they died and he was the lucky inheritor of the whole mess.

That night was the worst of his life – when he realized he hadn't just lost his parents; he was losing everything his family stood for. Still living in the Big House, he'd gone over and over the printouts the accountant gave him, looking for any good news in all the bad. Sometime around 2:30 in the morning, he'd gone to the kitchen to refill his drink and he'd taken in the granite countertops, high end appliances and hand quarried slate floor. He'd been surrounded by his mothers' excesses all this time and never thought to question it.

In that moment, the dim light of the refrigerator spilling across the floor, he had the awful thought that maybe his parents' deaths weren't an accident after all. Maybe broken under the load of debt, his father had deliberately crossed the line on the highway and driven off the road.

No. He knew that wasn't right. He knew it.

But the thought haunted him for days. It was with him when he confessed to Lacey the state of the ranch. It rung in his brain when she recoiled from him, ran away and refused to take his calls. Stuck in his head when he began to hear the rumors that she'd taken up with another man – a rich outsider come to town to buy a show ranch.

It kept him up through long nights of imagining that stranger touching her – sleeping with her. Prevented him from eating, and brought up whatever food he managed to choke down, while he struggled to find a foothold in the mountain of debt that would allow him to keep the ranch – and a reason to keep on trying now that Lacey had abandoned him. He wanted to throttle his father. Why hadn't he stood up to his mother? Why hadn't he stopped her?

Why hadn't he taken Ethan with them in the car that day, instead of leaving him to face this all on his own?

Driven by that last awful thought, he'd finally sought out Joe Halpern in town, the pastor of his parents' church – the one he hadn't attended in years – and let the whole thing spill out of him. Joe's words had been a kindness to him that day and they'd stuck with him ever since.

"Your father wasn't a quitter, Ethan. He worked hard every day because he saw opportunity around every corner. He loved your mom, maybe a little too much since it seems to have knocked the sense right out of him, but love does that sometimes. And that's okay, because in the end that's all that matters. You'll find a way to turn things around, and even if you don't, you'll be all right, because in the end it's the people in our lives, not the things we own, that make life worth living."

He wasn't sure if he agreed with that last part, but Joe was right about his father. Alex Cruz wasn't a quitter, and if he'd let his wife overspend it was because he adored her and wanted her to be happy. He must have thought he'd be able to recoup those costs and pay down that debt. And if he thought so, there must be a way. Ethan just had to find it.

Even if he did, that wouldn't fix the problem of the woman sleeping it off in his bedroom. A wave of heat ran through him although the air was still cool. She was something else. A beautiful, hot, curvaceous, willing woman who'd flown all this way simply to be with him. To join her whole life to his.

Always and forever.

The thought revved him up more than he wanted to admit.

Could it work?

No way. The whole thing was preposterous – outrageously stupid. If he'd learned anything in the past eight months, surely it was not to trust a beautiful woman. Or fate.

He had to sit her down, explain the whole thing, wipe away her tears and put her on that plane.

Autumn awoke with a start.

Something was wrong. Something was really, really wrong.

As she did a mental inventory, her stomach pulled into a sickening knot and the back of her throat ached.

Was she hurt? No, but she didn't feel exactly normal...down there.

Where was she? In her apartment? No, and not at a hotel either. In a man's bedroom, in...*Ethan's* bedroom.

And it all came back in a rush. Arriving by plane, acting her part, going to DelMonaco's, Rob announcing their engagement to all and sundry, the drinks, more drinks, more drinks, and then....

Oh no.

No. She couldn't have. She...ohmygod she was naked and...oh, yeah, she'd definitely had sex.

With a stranger.

Without protection.

Shit.

She sat up and the whole world swum around her as she clutched the comforter to her chest. Where were her clothes, dammit? No, scratch that – where was the washroom?

She dashed across the room and just made it before she heaved what was left in her stomach from the previous night's alcoholic romp. Slamming the bathroom door shut with her foot, she blotted her mouth with toilet paper, flushed the toilet, and knelt on the cold, tile floor, wanting to lay down and die.

Why, oh why hadn't she told Ethan he needed to use a condom? Much to her gynecologist mother's disgust, Autumn couldn't tolerate birth control pills and had discontinued them after several years of battling migraines. In the past she'd simply spoken up to her boyfriends about her need to use an alternate form of protection. She wasn't embarrassed about it. Her only excuse for last night's lapse was she was too drunk to think straight...and out of practice.

"Use protection. Every. Single. Time." Her mother's words – uttered at least once a week during her teenage years – rang in her mind.

How much more proof did she need that she was a complete and total failure? Not only would she go back to New York without the story she so desperately needed, she might return knocked up. She could picture her mother and sister's reactions.

Autumn screws up again. Autumn never finishes what she starts. Autumn's having a baby. At 24. Before she even gets her career off the ground.

Failure. Complete and total failure.

She forced herself to her feet, gripping the countertop when the room swam again. It was stark and practical – white tiles, a Formica counter, plain Jane mirror cabinet and fixtures. A man's razor was plugged into an outlet and a can of shaving cream sat nearby. A bar of soap and tube of toothpaste near the sink. Forest green towel and washcloth. The bathroom of a man who didn't waste time or thought on home décor. A cowboy's bathroom.

She ran cold water in the sink and splashed her face, wiping away the tears she hadn't realized she was crying. No, she wouldn't let her family down or herself down – not again. What were the chances she'd gotten pregnant from just one time? More likely she'd caught some stupid disease – hopefully not a deadly one. She'd haul her ass into a doctor as soon as she was able and get checked out.

She'd grit her teeth, finish out this assignment, get her photos and get the hell back to New York. And if she was pregnant she'd deal with it. There were answers to every problem.

Grabbing the washcloth, she scrubbed at her face viciously until all traces of tears were gone, then swished some toothpaste around her mouth as best she could. As she retraced her steps to the bedroom, and began to search for her clothes, she refused to listen to the voice that told her if she was pregnant, she'd never give up the child.

Ethan walked into the bedroom as Autumn was pulling on a pair of panties. She swiveled around in surprise and with a small cry clamped one arm across her chest, but not before he got a good look at a part of her anatomy that had enthralled him the night before.

He stopped, cleared his throat and searched for something to say. "Good morning."

She stared at him. "Uh…morning." Her voice was shrill and high, and he realized she wasn't entirely comfortable with the situation. Somehow that made him grin. He wasn't comfortable with this situation, either – not by a long shot – but her current position, half-naked, her arm doing very little to cover the curve of her assets, was fine by him. He could watch this show all morning.

"Do you mind?" she said finally.

He leaned back against the doorjamb. "Not at all. Go ahead."

"I'm not getting dressed while you stand there!"

She was blushing again, and it looked even better on her this time than it had the night before. He allowed himself a long look. What a body. Long legs, shapely hips dipping in to a small waist and then the swell of her breasts. He definitely approved.

"Why not? You're my fiancée, right?"

He knew he was being a cad. After all, he was about to break the news about the joke. So why was he pushing her like this? Almost daring her to say it wasn't true. But he was the one who was lying – she was here because she wanted to marry him. Wasn't she?

Suddenly Ethan wanted to know that for sure. Was she really here because one look at his video hooked her for life? Her actions seemed to back up that theory. She'd been willing to sleep with him a scant few hours after she'd arrived, but then again he'd been pretty willing, too, and he had no intention of marrying her.

He waited. After a long moment, she nodded. "Right."

"So get dressed. I want to see what I'm getting out of the bargain."

Her color deepened, but she took a deep breath, raised her chin, dropped her arm and spun in a circle. "This is what you're getting. Satisfied?"

There was an edge to her voice, so he shifted tactics. "I like what I see," he said. He pushed off the door frame and crossed the room. "But I'm not satisfied by a long shot." He bent down and captured her mouth with his, pulling her closer until those breasts that drove him wild pressed up against his bare chest. At first she resisted him. She slid her hands up between them and tried to push him away, but when he let his hand fall to the curve of her bottom and gave a gentle squeeze, she groaned and wrapped her arms around his neck.

As he maneuvered them toward the bed, Ethan remembered his resolve. Damn it, he was supposed to be sending her home, not seducing her a second time. "I…" he started, not sure at all what he was going to say. "I…need to get to work. It's late."

"What?" She was flushed and tousled and so beautiful he wanted to pitch her onto the bed and make love to her until neither of them could think straight.

"It's late. This is a ranch," he stammered. "I can't stay here – I've got to go…"

"Oh," she said, then seemed to comprehend. "Oh, right! The ranch. Sorry, I…I got distracted."

He laughed, "Honey, we both did." Honey? Did he just call her honey? Get a grip, Ethan – she's leaving on the first flight!

But even as he thought it, he knew it wasn't true. She wasn't going anywhere until he got to know her better. It was wrong to lie to her and let her believe he would go through with this…marriage…but there was nothing wrong with getting to know a pretty girl and seeing if they had what it took to get serious about each other. He'd suggest they back things off for the time being. Take it real slow. He'd say that while the marriage notion might have brought them together it was only fair to both of them that they think of this month as a series of dates. He'd suggest they move into separate bedrooms so she didn't feel pressured. They'd build a relationship one step at a time like normal people did. Then, if things went well, they might decide to take it to the next step. Either party could cancel at any time.

After all, he wanted to find a partner. He wanted a woman who wanted what he did; to build a successful life on the ranch that included a thriving business and a thriving family, as well. According to Rob, she wanted a country life, a strong man and lots of children. They had more in common than he did with most of the women he grew up with in Chance Creek.

He kissed her again, pulling away reluctantly. "Go on, get dressed. I'll show you around the house and grounds and then head out."

Autumn pulled on jeans, a t-shirt, and socks and swept her hair up into a sensible pony-tail. She found her tooth brush and mouthwash, and felt much better after another trip to the washroom. When she made her way to the kitchen, Ethan presented her with a plate filled with toast, sausage and fried eggs. A glance at the table told her he'd made himself an identical breakfast. Too bad she was half his weight and still suffering from that hangover. She wasn't sure she could keep down a bite, let alone clean this plate.

"I swear this is the last time," he said, gesturing to the meal. "My mom hated men in her kitchen – I bet you do, too. There should be enough food kicking around in the fridge and cabinets for a day or so. You just make me a list and I'll pick up any supplies you need when I go into town tomorrow. Your domain, I swear. I won't intrude."

"Uh…thanks." Since when did women mind men making breakfast for them? She loved puttering in the kitchen, but had no problem sharing the job with someone else. What kind of person was his mother – a total control freak? She glanced out the back screen door and relaxed. Probably the work he did out there consumed all his time and then some. And it sounded like he'd leave her to it and not micro-manage the way she handled the chore. She appreciated that. She'd dated a chef once – Erik Whittleton – and the one time she made herself toast in his kitchen he'd nearly blown a fuse. That had ended things between them. She loved to cook, and if Ethan wanted her to take over the kitchen while she was here, she'd be more than happy to oblige.

Ethan took a bite of sausage and followed it with a scoop of egg. "I'll be gone most of the day. I'll cut out early, though, and try to be back around five o'clock and we can have dinner together. How's that sound?"

Five o'clock? What was it – about half past six in the morning right now? "What do I do all day?"

"Well, you can cook me dinner," he said, grinning. "Anything with meat. Otherwise, look around the place and get settled. Relax."

She bit her lip. "You said in your video you're looking for a woman to help you run the ranch. Sitting around all day doesn't sound that useful." Plus it wouldn't get her any photographs of handsome cowboys roping cattle – or whatever it is one did on a ranch in Montana.

"Hmm." Ethan considered this. "I need to cover a lot of ground today – Jamie and I are checking the fence on the south pasture, so it's not a great time for you to tag along. If you're ready to help out you can always work on the kitchen garden, though. It's in pretty sad shape. Mom used to feed us out of it most of the time. I don't know what you can salvage this year, but anything you can do would be great. I promise I'll

58

take you out with me on a day's work soon, though – let you get an idea of what we do here."

"Okay." She'd prefer to spend today with him, and shoot some pictures of him checking those fences, but she didn't want to scare him off by being too pushy. It seemed like he hadn't put a whole lot of thought into her arrival. If she hadn't known better, she'd think he'd been surprised by it. What kind of guy roped a woman into marriage, then tried to feed her takeout food, didn't give her a ring, and ditched her on her first full day in town? Maybe this was why he had to use the internet to get a wife in the first place.

She resigned herself to sticking around the house. She decided she would use the opportunity to take some photographs of it and the surrounding area, too. Lots of them, in case she decided to bail early. She could always do a fluff piece on Montana ranch life. If she got bored, she'd work in that garden.

"Is Jamie your only ranch hand?"

"No, but he's the only one living on-site right now." He shrugged. "I didn't have anyone to run the place – do the cooking and all that – and as you can see, I'm living in the bunk house. I didn't feel much like living in the Big House once my parents passed on. Most of the men live nearby. They drive in each day."

He ate his sausages in two bites and mopped up the remainder of the egg with half a slice of toast. "Gotta run. Sorry to leave you in the lurch." He stood up and she did, too, trailing him to the door. He hesitated, one hand on the handle. "I'm glad you came.

We'll talk more tonight, work out all the details." He bent down and gave her another kiss that sent shivers of desire down to her toes.

"Okay," she managed to say, and watched him disappear out the back door and around the corner of the house.

As she stepped back into the kitchen and looked around, she got the feeling leaving Ethan when the time came might end up being much more difficult than she had expected. No other man made her lose control with the slightest touch. If he'd wanted to take her right here on the kitchen table, she'd have swept the dishes onto the floor herself. What was there about him that made her want to leap into his arms and give herself up to his command? Was she losing her mind? Had worry about her career completely unhinged her?

She cleared the table, swept her leftovers into the trash and filled the sink with soapy water, exploring the kitchen as she went to figure out where everything belonged. It was spare but adequate and while her mother might look down on the plain board counter tops and linoleum floor, she had a feeling this room had seen a lot of life and had many stories to tell. As a teller of stories herself, she felt a kinship to the room she'd never felt with any of her city apartments.

It was just a month, she thought. What if she allowed herself the fantasy of being a farm wife to the sexiest cowboy alive? She could sew gingham curtains for the windows, bake comfort food every night, rub his back at bedtime, and...sleep with him?

Could she sleep with a man for a month and then walk out?

Well, why not? She'd had other short term relationships that started with a bang and then fizzled out fast. She hadn't planned them ahead of time, but she'd lived through them and no one was worse for wear. She could do it.

She dropped a hand to her belly, then jerked it away. That was just stupid. Even if she was pregnant, she wouldn't be able to tell for weeks, and by then she'd be well on her way back to New York. No sense getting her panties in a wad about something that wasn't even on the radar.

She scrubbed the counters, swept the floor and admired her handiwork. She'd plan a menu for the week this afternoon and ask about curtain material when Ethan got home. For now, she was going to take advantage of this break from her normal life, grab her camera and head outside.

Chapter Four

Ethan looked up as soon as he felt the shudder of hoofbeats heading his way.

"Rob's coming," Jamie said. "Looks like he's got Cab with him."

Ethan turned his back on the approaching horsemen and returned to resetting a fallen fencepost in its hole. He welcomed the chore today as a chance to get out into open country and think about his situation. He didn't need Rob around to taunt him, as well.

"Get any sleep?" Rob hollered as he rode up on his chestnut quarter horse, Monty.

Ethan didn't answer. He hoped Rob would get the message and keep on riding, but Rob being Rob, it didn't happen that way.

"Did you sleep at all? I bet the springs in that mattress of yours got quite a workout." He made creaking noises until Ethan stood up and fixed him with a glare. Cab kept quiet, but he could tell he was working hard to suppress a smile.

"Stow it."

"Come on, admit it – we picked you a good wife, didn't we? So, you gonna keep her or are you putting her back on that plane?"

"I'm putting her back on the plane."

Rob scratched his neck and made a show of looking around. "This don't look like no airport, buddy. She's going to miss her flight."

"She's not leaving today." Suddenly he found it hard to look Rob in the eye. Jamie stood up from where he'd been running a new wire, and came closer.

Cab cocked his head. "She's leaving but she's not leaving?"

"Let me get this straight," Rob drawled. "You dumped her, and she decided to stick around for a visit?" He felt Rob's assessing look. "Oh, I get it. You haven't told her yet, have you? You figure you'll keep her around for a few days, bang her a few more times, and then let her down easy. Real smooth, cowboy."

"That's not how it is at all." Damn it, couldn't a man get a moment to think things through before people came poking around and telling him what's what? Jamie had the good sense to keep his mouth shut all morning – too bad Rob couldn't be like him. "I'm not going to keep banging her." Shit. That didn't come out right.

All three men laughed. "I knew you'd had a good roll in the hay last night," Rob said. "Hell, the two of you were practically hitting home base in the truck. So, how was it?"

"Get the hell outta here."

"No. I'm not done with you yet. Look, you like Autumn. She's hot, she likes you, she wants everything you have to offer. Why the hell would you send her home?"

"Seems kind of stupid to me," Jamie put in. Even Cab was nodding.

He stifled the urge to kick the fence post. No sense having to do the job over twice. "I'm not sending her home right away." He ran a hand through his hair. "Look, I'm going to slow this down. I'm going to try to get to know her like normal people do before I jump back into the sack with her."

Rob cocked his head. "Get to know her? Buddy, I think you got to know her pretty good last night. Just how do you plan to get to know her better?"

Ethan turned back to his work. "I don't know. Move her into the spare room, set some ground rules."

More laughter all around.

Rob urged his horse forward. "You think you can put her in the spare room and pretend you two just met? Ain't going to work. I bet you ten to one you're back in the saddle with her tonight. Hell, probably before lunch. Don't forget, you two are getting married in 29 days. I've already booked the chapel."

"What do you mean, you booked…"

Cab leaned over his saddle. "We got lucky. Some out of town couple canceled for June 21st. Hell of a coincidence, eh?"

"Coincidence, my ass," Ethan said. He couldn't believe Rob had persuaded the normally sane sheriff to be a part of this farce. "Don't you all think this joke has gone too far?" He looked from one to another of his friends' much too cheerful faces.

"You saying you want us to take her to the airport today?" Jamie said slowly. "Because if you're that sick of her I'm more than willing to take her off of your hands."

Just like that, Ethan saw red. He took a step forward. "You stay away from her!"

They were laughing at him again before he even managed to spit the words out.

"Admit it, Ethan – you're hooked on her," Rob howled.

Ethan shook his head and went back to work.

Autumn hoped like hell she was pulling the weeds and not the vegetables. Regardless of what she'd said in her video, she'd never really gardened, unless you called repotting a begonia now and then on her apartment's balcony gardening. Luckily, it was far enough into the growing season that the plants looked like plants. She'd already gotten through two rows of the large kitchen garden and was partway through a third when hoofbeats pounded up behind her and she scrambled to her feet.

Brushing the dirt from her knees, she shaded her eyes and was surprised at the dip of disappointment in her stomach when she realized it wasn't Ethan, but one of his friends – Rob.

"Howdy!" he said, pulling up a few feet from the garden.

"Howdy? Do people really say that?"

"Yes, Ma'am, they do." Most women would call Rob handsome, but something about him set her teeth on edge . When he and Ethan talked, tension ran between them like an electric fence. Something was wrong between them, so the fact he'd come to visit when Ethan was out put up her guard. He slid from the saddle and tossed the horse's reins to the ground.

"Won't he run off?"

"No, Ma'am, not Monty." Rob smiled and came closer. "Just talked to Ethan. Sounds like you two had a hell of a night."

She felt the heat rise in her cheeks. Ethan had been bragging to Rob? Just what had he said?

"Oh, he didn't share the details," Rob said as if reading her mind. "I inferred them from the glazed look in his eye and a certain hitch in his step."

Now she was really blushing. Damn it, who was this cowboy to stand here and talk to her like this? "Is there anything I can do for you?" She hoped the chill in her voice would back him off. She was enjoying her time in the garden and didn't really appreciate the interruption. She'd spent several hours wandering in ever-widening circles around the grounds and taken dozens of photographs with her digital camera of the landscape, the distant river and mountains, and the various buildings on the property – especially the pretty big log house that sat on a rise of land just a few hundred feet away. Ethan's real home, she assumed. The one he'd lived in before his parents died.

"Nah, this is just a social call. We westerners are mighty social, you know. It gets lonely working on these big spreads, so we like to mix things up. Visit each other. Ask each other in for a drink of lemonade and a slice of cake." He trailed off, obviously waiting for his invitation.

Well, he wasn't getting one. Regardless of his over-friendly tone – actually, because of it – she had the feeling Rob was looking for trouble. Probably thought she was easy, coming out here and hooking up with a stranger her first night in town. Maybe he thought he could get lucky, too. Or maybe he somehow sensed her scam, she thought with a sudden chill. Maybe he was here to investigate.

"Look. I don't know you from Adam and I'm not inviting you inside for a piece of…cake. Why don't ride on into the sunset and let me get back to work."

"Whoa, honey, I think you've misunderstood my intentions. I'm just trying to help things between you and Ethan along. I think the two of you are a match made in heaven. I'm not trying to rustle his cattle."

She didn't know what part of that declaration to take offense at first. "Okay, first of all, I'm not a cow. I'm a woman, in case you haven't noticed. Second, what do you mean you're trying to help things along? What exactly needs helping here? He put out a video, I answered it. Here I am. Here I'm staying. We'll be married in a month." She put her hands on her hips and tried to look like an aggrieved fiancée.

"Slow down. I never called you a cow. I am definitely aware you are a woman. I think every man in the county is aware of that." He smiled in a way that made her squirm. "As for you and Ethan, you're exactly right; he put out an ad and you answered it. Heck, we've even booked the chapel for the 21st. But whether you actually get married is up to you, isn't it? Ethan's got 29 days to change his mind. If I were you, I'd put some thought into how to keep him on track, and while tending the garden is all well and good, I'd spend some time tending...Ethan...if you know what I mean."

They'd booked the chapel? She only spared a moment on that unsettling tidbit before moving on to the next thing Rob said. Tending Ethan? Ethan changing his mind? "What did he say?" The thread of fear in her voice was no act. If Ethan was losing interest, she had no story. She needed the whole shebang – the back story, the courtship, the ring, wedding preparations...

"He likes you, honey. He really does. But he thinks you want to take things slow. He said he got the impression you wanted to move into the guest room and go back to holding hands until you get to know each other better. And that's not what he asked for in his video, is it? He asked for a wife. You don't win a man like Ethan through conversation. You win him through his stomach and his...well, you know. Food and sex. That's what counts."

He climbed back into the saddle and turned Monty around. "He's in the south pasture. Take the truck – keys are in the ignition – and follow that track." He pointed. "Head out a couple of miles. You can't miss it."

"What are you talking about?"

"Food and sex!" Rob hollered back at her as he urged Monty into a gallop. "You'll figure it out!"

Ethan was gathering his tools up when he heard the sound of a truck's engine. A familiar engine. What the hell? That was his Ford F-250 inching its way along the track toward him. A sudden lurch of fear had his heart beating double-time. Was something wrong with Autumn? Was she hurt?

Did she want to leave?

He forced himself to wait while the truck slowed to a halt and the engine died. Jamie had returned to the barn to care for the horses, Cab needed to get to work and he assumed Rob had gone to work with his father and brothers on his own spread, though he hadn't said anything specific. The door opened and one long, bare leg appeared, then another. Autumn slid to the ground and smoothed her form-fitting flowered cotton sundress down. "I brought a picnic," she called, and hauled a basket down from the truck heavy enough to nearly unbalance her. She held it with two hands and made her way over to him.

He couldn't take his eyes off the button between her breasts or the expanse of skin above it. Was she wearing anything under that dress? It didn't look like it.

"Where should we eat?" She planted her feet in front of him and leaned back to counterbalance the weight of the basket, looking at him expectantly.

"Uh…" *Damn it, man, pull yourself together.* He pointed to an pine tree that offered some shade from the heat of the midday sun. "How about over there?" He had the presence of mind to take the basket from her - hell, what was in there – bricks? – and led the way. She caught up with him after a couple of steps and slid her hand into his.

That one small gesture nearly undid him. He found his own fingers tightening around hers and a smile creeping across his face that he quickly squashed. They were supposed to be slowing things down – getting to know each other like normal people.

Normal people held hands, didn't they?

Sure, but his reaction to her touch was anything but innocent.

When they reached the tree, Autumn took the basket back, set it down and opened the lid. Ethan felt like he'd entered a dream as she spread out a blanket and pulled out dish after dish. She set two places with a couple of chipped china plates, and cloth napkins she'd found who knew where. She'd brought fried chicken, sandwiches, pickles, chips, hard boiled eggs, potato salad, even a homemade peach cobbler. She poured a glass of lemonade and handed it to him.

"I thought you might be starving out here."

"Thanks." Was that his voice? He was starving, all right, but it wasn't food he needed.

He sat down just the same and ate his fill, noticing she was watching him from under her lashes. She seemed nervous, plying him with food every time there was room on his plate, refilling his glass before he could empty it. She barely ate or drank a thing.

"What's wrong?" he asked finally. She was making him nervous, too. What if this was some kind of last supper – a little treat before she dumped him and asked for cab fare back to the airport?

"Nothing, I just…Ethan, are you happy I'm here?"

He placed a chicken leg back on the plate. "Yes. Why?"

"It's just…I don't know. I came all the way here, and we had a good time last night, and then you just left…I didn't know if you'd gotten sick of me already."

"Sick of you?" He shook his head. "No. Of course not. This is a ranch, honey – the work here doesn't take a holiday." He wished it would. Lord knew, he could spend all day exploring Autumn's body, making sweet love to her until…

She hesitated, her fingers in her lap worrying each other until he wanted to reach across and take both of them in his. "You're sure you're not sick of me?"

"No. Definitely not."

She took a breath, looked up at him and said, "Prove it."

Ethan's eyebrows shot for his hairline. "Prove it?" *Damn, stop repeating what she says, you sound like an ass!* "How?"

He held his breath. Here's where her true motivations would show themselves. Maybe she was like his mother, all wrapped up in material possessions. Watch, she'd ask him to buy her that ring he'd promised her and when he took her to town she'd pick the biggest rock in the place.

"Make love to me."

At first he didn't understand her words. He'd been so prepared for disappointment he was already forming the phrases to let her know he couldn't be bribed with peach cobbler to buy her with jewelry, and Autumn's simple plea didn't even register. She said it again.

"Ethan, please make love to me."

With a growl of pure, primordial desire, he swept away the dishes, swooped her into his arms and laid her down on the blanket. He had to stop for a moment and take in the vision of this beautiful woman flushed with wanting him, waiting for his kiss, his touch. She'd cooked all morning and come out here to find him with the sole objective of seducing him, he realized. He felt like the cares of the world had been lifted off of his shoulders. She wasn't anything like Lacey, or his mother. She wasn't hiding anything, she didn't have any ulterior motives. She wanted him for him and she wouldn't make him seek or beg or wait for her love. She would give it to him freely – more than he'd ever hoped for.

"Autumn." It was all he could say. Then he was kissing her, the fire between them scorching his lips. He felt her arms slide around his shoulders and her breasts pressing against his chest and his ardor heightened, until he had to get closer.

She must have felt the same, because she slid a palm up his chest and broke their kiss. "Wait." She gently pushed him back, then slowly, ever so slowly, began to undo the buttons of her dress.

As he'd suspected, she wore nothing beneath it. She spread the panels of fabric, exposing the beauty of her body to him, and he couldn't help but worship it. First with his hands, running them up and down, from her breasts, to her hips, to the warmth between her legs, then with his mouth, tracing passages up and down her curves and dips, landing finally where it could do the most good.

She arched in pleasure as he found her secret folds and teased and stroked her to heights that had her moaning aloud. Then, when he couldn't stand it anymore, he pushed himself into position above her and waited for her assent.

"Wait – just a second." She reached out blindly, patted her cast off dress until she found a pocket and pulled out a small packet. A condom.

Of course. Good thing one of them was thinking straight today. They barely knew each other – certainly not well enough to have unprotected sex, no matter what they'd gotten up to last night. He had the package open and the condom on in a matter of moments, and she pulled him close again, guiding him into her, opening herself to him and crying aloud as he thrust himself inside her and joined them as one.

With a cry of animal desire that shocked her as much as it thrilled her, she gripped Ethan's hips and urged him inside her. When he answered with a powerful thrust it was all she could do not to give herself up to oblivion right then.

She wanted more, though – much more. She didn't think she'd ever get enough of this man who filled her and set her on fire. If she'd known sex could be like this she'd have been combing Montana years ago, searching for her cowboy. New York would never be the same when she went back.

All thoughts rushed from her mind as Ethan's strokes brought her closer and closer to the edge. The male scent of sweat and leather, the softness of the blanket and hard, lumpy ground beneath her skin, blue sky and sunshine peeking between far overhead boughs all merged together in a blinding flash of heat and light as she swept over the edge of desire and into the abyss of ecstacy.

As they lay panting, entwined, Autumn's senses came back to her with a snap and with them came uncertainty. What kind of a person was she, using sex to secure a story? Maybe Ethan wasn't handing over cash, but she depended on her writing for a living, so in a way she was still trading sex for money as if she were a prostitute.

Although, if she was truthful, the story was the last thing on her mind right now. She tried to take a mental step back. What if there was no job on the line, what if she'd just met Ethan through friends or at a bar or party? Would she still be here, making love to him under the sun?

Yes. Oh, hell yes.

The answer came as clear as day, and with it an even greater sorrow. Because she couldn't have feelings for Ethan. He was nothing but a story to her, and in less than a month she had to get on a plane and leave for good. Once the story was published, there was no going back. He wouldn't want her then.

Ethan rolled off her and spooned her into an embrace. "Autumn, you are the best thing that's ever happened to me." He nuzzled her neck and breathed a contented sigh. For a few moments there was silence between them as they both gazed up at the blue sky winking in and out between the boughs of the pine. Then he whispered, "Autumn. Will you be my wife?"

She held her breath. *Oh my God, was that a real proposal?* In a flash she saw the month ahead, the ring, the congratulations, the parties, the preparations, the dress, the wedding…

No, not the wedding. She would leave before the wedding.

He was offering her everything she needed for this story – all the details she could use to write the kind of attention-getting, sexy, catty, zinging expose CityPretty demanded for its feature articles. As soon as she saw Ethan's video want ad for a bride, she knew she could use it as the basis for a scathing editorial on the lengths men would go to get exactly what they wanted.

So why was she hesitating? What had her boss told her time and time again? You can't be a journalist and have feelings – not when you work for a magazine like CityPretty. You have to go for the jugular, do what it takes to get the killer headline. Be ruthless! Feelings are for social workers.

"Autumn? Will you marry me?" Ethan asked again.

She took a breath.

"Yes."

Ethan waited while Autumn finished snapping photos of the partially weeded garden, the picnic basket sitting on the back steps – she fussed a little about not having any shots of his proposal, but agreed with him it was for the best since they were both in their birthday suits – and the mess she'd left in the kitchen when she'd raced off to find him. Together they washed up and straightened the kitchen and then he took her hand.

"Ready to go pick out that ring?"

She nodded hesitantly.

"You don't look so sure. Changed your mind already?" A stab of fear pierced his heart. He hoped she hadn't.

A small smile touched her lips. "It's not that, it's just...it feels weird, you spending money on me. It doesn't seem right. You hardly know me."

"I know I'm going to spend the rest of my life with you." A new thought struck him. "You know that, right? Marriage for me is forever. I don't do divorce."

Her eyebrows rose, delicate swoops of brown he longed to kiss. "I know. I feel that way, too. It's just...I don't want you to feel like you have to...buy things for me."

Her discomfort was plain to see and he wondered what had happened in the past to make her so hesitant to take a gift from a man. "Sweetheart, it's my job to take care of you now. I'm going to be your husband. I will spend the rest of my days making sure you have a roof over your head, food in your stomach and pretty clothes and jewelry to wear. There may be hard times now and then, and I may not be able to give you everything you want, but I will do my damnedest to see you right."

Her mouth fell open a little, and he was torn by the desire to kiss those soft lips and tear the man limb from limb who made this woman so shocked that someone might want to lighten her load.

"Come on, we're going to get you the prettiest ring you ever saw. Nothing but the best for my girl." He pulled her along out to the truck and had a sudden flash of understanding about his own parents. No wonder his father had put up with his mother's spending without a fight. He'd loved her to distraction – he'd wanted her happy, and so he did whatever it took to make sure she stayed that way, even if it meant mortgaging the ranch to the hilt.

Speaking of which.

Ethan realized in a rush of panic that he didn't have the money to buy a fancy engagement ring. What the hell was he thinking? As Autumn strapped herself into the passenger seat of the truck, he walked around to the driver's side slowly, cursing the amnesia that seemed to hit every time he was within five feet of her. Hell, he'd dug himself a good hole, hadn't he? He opened the door, climbed in, stuck the key in the ignition, and tried to breathe.

His credit cards were maxed out. He had barely enough cash to pay the bills until the next cattle sales went through. All his high-falutin' words about caring for Autumn and keeping her in house and health swirled in his mind. Empty promises. He was one flat tire away from going bankrupt himself.

What the hell was he going to do?

"Forget something?" Autumn said when he didn't start the truck.

"What? Yeah…yeah, I did. Hold on." He grabbed the excuse she handed him gratefully, hopped back out of the truck and retraced his steps to the house. Back inside the kitchen he pulled out his cell phone and dialed Rob.

"Rob. I need five thousand dollars. Now. For the ring, you rich sonofabitch. Move the money into my account. You have half an hour. Don't give me that – you're the one who booked the chapel, remember? Now I have to buy Autumn a ring. Yeah, so what if I like her; it's still your fault."

He hung up, knowing that for all Rob's intrinsic pain-in-the-assness, he was a friend he could count on in a pinch.

He tried to stifle the thought that he'd just dug his hole a little deeper. Worse, he was planning to enter the state of matrimony with a lie the size of Montana on his mind.

"That one." Autumn pointed to a thin silver ring dotted with the tiniest diamond chip she'd ever seen.

The salesgirl, whom Ethan had addressed as Rose, looked at them with a frown. "Really? You want to try that one?"

"It's nice, isn't it?" she asked Ethan innocently. She was not going to allow this man to spend a lot of money on her, story or no story, and when she secured her contract she would pay him back for the ring, just as soon as she could afford it... which unfortunately wouldn't be anytime soon.

Ethan looked at the ring and frowned. In fact, he hadn't looked comfortable since they'd climbed into the truck. Maybe he was having second thoughts. He glanced at his watch for what seemed like the fifth time in the past two minutes. "I think we need to take our time. I want you to try on every ring in the place until we find the right one."

"Why don't you tell me your price range," Rose said, "so I can help you stay under budget. That way your bride-to-be doesn't have to try so hard to spare your pocket." She winked at Autumn.

Ethan hesitated, and for the first time Autumn realized he must actually be on a budget. Maybe that was the real reason he'd left the Big House and moved into the bunkhouse. Maybe the Big House cost too much to keep up. Was the ranch losing money? She found that hard to believe – it looked prosperous enough. Although what did she know about cattle? She made a mental note to do some more research on the internet when she got home. She'd been too busy learning about horses and Montana to focus on the financials of running a ranch.

"Five thousand," he said, after a long moment.

Five thousand? It wasn't a huge budget, but it was nothing to sneeze at. Sure, lots of women spent more – way more – on their rings, but five grand certainly bought more than a diamond chip. Did he think she was such a princess she would look down on him for keeping to that amount? What kind of women lived out here in Montana if $5,000 was regarded as cheap? He caught her eye and she thought she detected a faint reddening to the skin on his neck and cheeks. Ethan was blushing? Over five thousand dollars?

"That's way too much," she said, shaking her head.

Cora Seton

"What's way too much?" The door slammed shut behind her, making her jump, and in an instant Rob was next to her at the counter, examining the rings in the glass cabinet as if he was the groom instead of Ethan.

"Hey, Rob," Rose said. "Ethan was just telling us his budget for the ring was five thousand dollars."

"Five thousand! Don't be a cheapskate, Ethan – buy the girl a real ring!"

"Rob," Ethan growled. "Get out of here."

"Don't worry, I'm not staying. Just wanted to say hi to my best girl, Rose." He leaned over the counter, and gave the petite brunette a resounding smack, "and to let your fiancée here know that you can afford to pay ten thousand dollars for a ring. Ten thousand. Got that, buddy? Rose, what do you think about these two? A match made in heaven?" He grinned, cocking an eyebrow.

"They'll do just fine," she said.

"Hear that, buddy?" he said to Ethan. "You're golden! Rose knows these things."

"Rob." Ethan grabbed him and hustled him toward the door. Autumn watched him haul the man out to the sidewalk.

"What's that all about?" she said.

Rose grinned. "Oh, Ethan and Rob have been friends all their lives. You'd think they could just give each other a man hug once in a while, but not them; they torment each other."

"What do you mean?"

"They play practical jokes all the time. If you ask me, though, Rob deserves some tormenting. If Ethan says five thousand, I'd stick to five thousand." She shrugged.

"Why does Rob deserve tormenting?"

Rose glanced around the store and leaned closer over the cabinet. "My friend Stacey heard from her friend Ella that her cousin was in town and met Rob at a bar. They were drinking and dancing all night and she went home with him." She lowered her voice even more. "Normally, I'd say a girl like that got what's coming to her, but no one deserves what Rob had planned. When they got to his bedroom he had a video camera set up – like, on a tripod! He'd hung a backdrop on one wall – painted like a barn with horses all around it and he had these lights set up. He wanted her to make a movie with him! A sex movie!"

Rose hissed the last words and Autumn's eyebrows shot up in surprise. So she'd been right about Rob – he was sleazy. Good thing she hadn't invited him inside this morning.

"What did he mean that you know things?"

Rose blushed. "Oh, don't mind him. It's just…" she fussed with some brochures near the register, "I get a feeling sometimes. About people. Couples. Whether they'll make it or not."

"Really?" Autumn did her best, but she was sure her face reflected her skepticism.

"It's nothing, really." Rose glanced at the door, as if eager for Ethan to return.

"And you think we'll make it? Ethan and I?"

After a moment, she nodded. "Yeah. You'll make it."

Some psychic, Autumn thought, her lips twisting. She opened her mouth to question Rose further when the door banged open again and Ethan walked in, alone. "Sorry about that, ladies, just needed to take out the trash." He looked from one to the other. "What're you two talking about?"

"Nothing," she said.

"All right, no more distractions. Let's pick out a ring."

She felt in her handbag for her camera and drew it out. "Mind if I take a few pictures?"

That evening, Autumn sat at a desk in the spare bedroom, staring at the blank page on her laptop. She'd taken photos of the jewelry store, Rose holding a display of rings, and her own hand with the delicate, new engagement ring sparkling on her finger. Now she needed to write.

Ethan helped her move her bags into this room, although they agreed she'd share his bed when it came time for sleeping. Neither one of them could pretend anymore they were going to take it slow. He gallantly suggested she needed a place to herself to get away to sometimes.

She told Ethan she was an avid diarist, as well as scrapbooker, and she wanted to write down the events of the last 24 hours while they were still fresh – and that she greatly appreciated having her own room in which do so. In reality, she needed to begin her article, so that by the time she flew back to New York it would be ready to turn in.

Once they'd returned from shopping, they'd eaten a quiet dinner made from her picnic lunch leftovers, then sat for a time on the back porch watching the sunset. They'd kissed a little and snuggled a lot, all of which made her long to kick her laptop to the curb and head for bed with Ethan, but she had to remember this was just a story. The diamond on her finger wasn't hers. Her fiancé wasn't a fiancé, he was just some guy she was lying to for the worst of reasons.

Money.

Is this what her mother meant by taking care of herself and being independent? Somehow she didn't think so. Sure, she would advocate doing what was necessary to survive, but was this necessary?

I won't have a job if I don't write this article, and in order to write this article I have to stay and play this out.

Was that true? Or could she somehow make a killer story out of what little material she already had? She grabbed her camera and clicked back through the photographs she'd saved.

No. She might have enough for a filler piece – two or three paragraphs, at most – but it wouldn't make a feature story. For that she needed the whole shebang – a hook, the backstory – a complete picture of a lonely cowboy looking for a real cowboy wife.

While she was at it, she'd better make some notes about the questions she still needed answers to. Why did he run the YouTube ad? Why not look for love in his own home town? Why be a rancher at all? Why not join the 21st century and get a real job?

And did he really want kids?

When she realized she'd dropped her hand to her belly, she snatched it up like she'd touched hot coals.

Don't even think it, Autumn – you can't be pregnant. And you certainly can't know that you are.

But she did know. She was as sure of it as she was of her own name. The thought made her hot with longing and cold with shame and fear all at the same time. What was she going to do? What would her mother and sister say when she came home pregnant?

A single mother, just like her own mom. Would she be able to rise to the challenge? Could she work all day at whatever came to hand, and go back to school to get her Masters so she could teach like her mother always said she should? Her baby in daycare from morning to night.

That last thought made her arms ache. She wouldn't get to raise her own baby; not like she wanted to, anyway. She wouldn't be there to hold her, play with her, keep her safe. Bake her cookies, play house, teach her to garden…

She bowed her head in frustration. After she became an ob-gyn, her own mother claimed she'd always felt stifled as a stay-at-home mom, but although she never said so, Autumn remembered things differently. She remembered many happy times with her mother and sister. Teresa used to set the timer on the oven and all three of them would race to finish their chores on summer mornings so they could spend the remainder of the day at a local pool. When they visited museums and art galleries, they had passionate arguments over which painting or sculpture they liked best. Her mother read aloud to them every night before bed. And then there were Sundays, and the noisy, fabulous feasts she missed so much.

She couldn't believe Teresa hated those days. Instead, she thought her mother had decided to hate them, so the fact she'd lost them when her husband left wouldn't be so devastating.

That didn't mean Autumn couldn't have days like those.

The ring on her finger glinted.

She could stay here, marry Ethan, be his wife. He wanted a stay-at-home kind of woman, someone to run the house, do the errands, raise the garden and the kids, and help with the ranch. They could make each other's dreams come true.

Lord knew, it wouldn't be a hardship to go to bed with him every night.

No.

She found herself shaking her head, her mother's constant lectures echoing in her mind. That meant financial dependence on a man, and that was something she could not, *would not*, do. When you depended on a man you left your life open to earth-shattering changes – the kind that tore your heart out and stomped on it for good measure. She couldn't raise a daughter with that kind of example. Marriage was a trap laid for women by men. A financial trap. And she wouldn't be a party to it.

Write, she told herself. *Earn your money and secure the future, for yourself and your baby.*

Chapter Five

How long did it take to write in a damn diary?

Ethan hesitated outside the spare bedroom door, one hand raised to knock. He heard the clack of computer keys and for one horrible moment wondered if maybe Autumn's diary was one of those blog things. Hell, he hoped not. The last thing he needed was for details of his private life to be exposed to the world – especially the details of the last 24 hours.

"Autumn?" He rapped his knuckles on the door. "You still in there?"

"Uh…yeah!" He heard the snap of her laptop shutting and the pad of her feet as she approached the door. She opened it a crack.

"It's been an hour. You aren't sitting there telling our story to the whole world, are you?" He craned his neck to see into the room.

Her eyes went wide. "What?"

"You're not one of those bloggers, are you? Or one of those video people?"

She cocked her head. "You think I'm writing an online diary?"

"Are you?"

"No. I'm just emailing a friend."

"Can I come in?" She looked hot, peeking up at him like that. Just being this close to her made him want to touch her cheek, or better yet…

"Give me one minute to pack all this up and I'll meet you in the kitchen."

"How about meeting me in the bedroom?"

A tiny smile quirked her lips and desire raced through his bloodstream. "Let's meet in the kitchen first."

She shut the door gently but firmly, and he sighed, frustrated she didn't seem as eager to be with him as he was to be with her. He retreated to the kitchen and grabbed himself a beer from the fridge.

A minute later she joined him, taking a seat at the table. She looked nervous; she was playing with her new ring, twisting it around and around her finger.

"I know this is going to sound weird, and I don't want it to be, but I feel like I have to say it," she began.

Oh hell, if this was going where he thought it was going, he was just going to have to pack it in. First his parents' death, then the discovery of the debt, then Lacey's abandonment and now this woman, who'd managed to worm her way into his heart in less than 24 hours, was going to break up with him? And probably wanted to keep the ring for a souvenir?

"I don't think we should sleep together anymore until the wedding," she blurted out.

Ethan hesitated. That wasn't what he'd expected. Sure, he'd thought about slowing things down, too.

Hadn't he said as much to Rob? But that was before their picnic. "Come again?" he said.

"Sex. I don't think we should have sex until we're married." She bit her lip, her expression pleading with him to understand. To not get mad.

"Let me get this straight," Ethan finally said. "You came out here to get married. You had sex with me – made love to me – within hours of meeting me, and again at lunch time today. Why the sudden change of heart?"

"It's just…" she scanned the room as if looking for help. "It's just all backwards, you know? We're supposed to fall in love first, then get married, then make love."

Ethan's eyebrows shot for his hairline. "Are you really that traditional?"

She flushed. "No. Obviously not."

"Then what's really eating you?"

She shook her head. "I can't tell you."

A coil of unease tightened in Ethan's stomach. She was hiding something – something she knew he wouldn't want to know. Well, he wouldn't abide that kind of behavior. He took her hand and tugged it gently until she looked up at him.

"No secrets. That's my one rule for this marriage – everything else we can negotiate. Whatever it is you need to tell me you tell me right now. I won't bite. I may be angry, I may not; depends on what you're hiding. But I won't hurt you – we'll figure it out."

She shook her head again. "I can't."

"Autumn. Spill it."

Autumn sucked in a breath. There was no denying the authority in that tone of voice. He'd guessed right away she was keeping a secret – now he wouldn't give in until she told him everything.

No. Not everything.

Just enough to distract him from her real secret.

"I think I'm pregnant."

Ethan's mouth opened, closed, then opened again. "You came here to marry me pregnant with someone else's baby?"

"What? No! Of course not. I haven't been with a man in three years!" Hysterical laughter bubbled up in her throat at this particular misunderstanding, but she clamped it back, knowing full well it wouldn't help her any. "I mean I'm...not on birth control. And we didn't use any protection that first time and...I feel different. I know it's too soon to tell. I know it's crazy, but I just...know. I'm sorry. I should have said something last night before we made love. It just happened so fast and I was drunk..."

He stood, knocking his chair to the floor. "You're not on birth control. And you didn't tell me? How many times have you done this?"

She sat back like she'd been slapped. "Done what?"

"Had unprotected sex with a stranger and then extorted money from him. Is that how you make your living? Is that what this is all about? You sleep around, get knocked up, gather diamond rings, then take off, get rid of the baby, and cash in?"

"No!" She stood, too. "How can you say that? I've never done anything like this before. I've never met anyone who made me lose my head, or...I just told you. I haven't been with another man in three years. I was waiting – waiting until I could take care of myself, so I wouldn't ever get stuck in a relationship with a man like you!"

"What do you mean, a man like me?"

"A selfish, arrogant, misogynistic control freak who'll steal the best years of my life, lure me into depending on him and then dump me the minute he finds someone younger and prettier."

She stormed out of the room and back to the spare bedroom, locking the door behind her. *That was fantastic, Autumn – way to keep the story going*. After this he'd kick her out for sure and then where would she be?

"Autumn." His voice was muffled through the solid bedroom door, but she could tell he was calmer now. "Open up. We have to talk this through. I'm sorry I yelled, but you can't blame me for being surprised."

"I don't want to talk."

"Well, sometimes we have to do things we don't want to do. Open the door."

There was that quiet authority again. It galled her, but she had to respect it and the impetus behind it to do the right thing. The adult thing.

Reluctantly, she crossed the room and turned the lock. When he entered the room, she retreated to the bed, tucking one leg under her and sitting as far from him as she could.

"I just want to know if I have this right. You aren't on the Pill."

She shook her head.

"And I didn't use protection last night. This is my fault as much as yours. At least you brought a condom with you at lunch today. I thought you were just worried about diseases."

She let out a breath. "I'm worried about everything. I don't know how to do this – I'm totally out of practice. I was afraid when I pulled out the condom you'd get mad."

Ethan's brows furrowed. "No – of course not. Like I said, I should have thought of it sooner. I'm kind of out of practice, too, I guess. Hell, we're lucky you even found me. This is a big ranch, you know. I could have been anywhere."

"It wasn't luck. Rob told me. He said…" She trailed off, not wanting to go there, but she was learning that Ethan was like a dog going after a bone when it came to finding out the truth.

"What did Rob tell you?"

There it was again, that implacable tone that made her feel about five years old. "He said the way to your heart was through your stomach and…you know." She waited for the storm of his anger, but it didn't come.

When she glanced up, Ethan was shaking his head, a strange expression on his face.

"Figures. Sweetheart, the way to my heart is through being yourself and telling me the truth. The whole truth. I'm looking for a partner, not some sex-crazed chef, although...now that I say that aloud, it doesn't sound half bad."

She threw the pillow at him.

He caught it easily and grinned. "So, let me get this straight. You were so worried about losing me, you baked all morning and then seduced me in the open air?"

Could she hide under the blankets? When he said it like that it sounded ridiculous. She pushed back against the headboard as he made his way across the room and sat down next to her on the bed. "And now you think you're pregnant?"

"I don't know. It's stupid, right? I couldn't possibly know." She ducked her head, unable to look him in the eye, but he took her chin in his hand and tilted it up. Before she could speak, his kiss cut off her words and despite everything, she found herself leaning into it. He gathered her up into his lap and in the safety of the circle of his arms, she let all her worries slip away as his mouth ravaged hers. She responded hungrily, unable to get enough of his attentions.

But when his hands skimmed up her waist to her breasts, she blocked his way and broke off the kiss. "No. Ethan, we can't keep doing this."

"Why not? If you're pregnant, it won't hurt the baby, and if you aren't, don't you think we should remedy that as soon as possible?"

Something melted within her. It was so hard to resist the touch of his hands, or his logic, but she fought her way to mental clarity. She was not marrying this man, could not marry anyone until she was financially stable on her own two feet. Her only hope was that she was mistaken and there was no baby. If they kept on the way they'd started she'd never be able to leave when it was time to go. She was already half-addicted to him and he was still a stranger.

"We have to wait."

"Why?" he growled into her neck from where he was placing kisses behind her ear, down her clavicle, under her chin.

"Because. We aren't married." She pushed him away. "There may be a ring on my finger but until we're married, I can't be absolutely sure about your intentions. Maybe it's too late, maybe there's already a baby growing inside me, but if there isn't it's time for me to be responsible." She wasn't sure her excuses would work – wasn't entirely sure she wanted them to.

He tapped his fingers on the comforter, clearly not happy with this turn of events. "We can be careful. I've got more condoms around here somewhere."

"Ethan, no." She held her breath.

With a sigh he lifted her off of his lap and stood up. "If you want to break off the engagement, just say so."

She should break it off right now. Keeping up this pretense was only going to hurt them both. But her job...where would she find a new one in this economy?

"I don't want to break it off. I just want to learn more about my future husband first. Is that so bad?"

"I guess not. Come on." He held out his hand.

She took it uncertainly. "Where are we going?"

He didn't answer. Instead he led her to the back porch, snagging a can of soda and another beer on his way through the kitchen. He popped open the soda, handed it to her, and indicated the swing. She sat down on one side and he sat down next to her, taking a swig of his own drink.

"We'll keep you off the booze until you know one way or the other about being pregnant. Meanwhile, what do you want to know?"

"Um..." Where was that list of questions when she needed it? "How old are you?"

"Twenty-eight."

Four years older than her. That sounded about right. "Did you go to college?"

"College?" He laughed. "You're looking at my university right here, Sweetheart. My parents died last summer, left the ranch to me. I'd worked it my whole life, but working it and running it turned out to be two different things."

"That's a huge responsibility. Don't you have any other family?"

"A sister. Claire. She wasn't interested in coming home to help."

"Oh." They swung in silence for a minute. "I always wanted one of those big extended families. You know, where everyone comes for the holidays and it's so noisy you can't even hear yourself think?"

He nodded. "Don't you have family?"

"Yep. My mom. A sister."

"Sounds like the makings of a big family."

"Neither are married, and my sister has no kids."

"Ah. Good thing we're starting early, then." He squeezed her hand. "We'll just have to have a dozen to make up for everyone else."

She stilled. "Would you really want a dozen kids?"

"If I could have them, I'd welcome every one."

If he could have them. Evidently he could have them, if Autumn was to be believed. Of course, it was silly to think she could know one way or the other. Women couldn't tell if they were pregnant within 24 hours of making love.

Could they?

He somehow trusted her when she said there hadn't been another man for years. He didn't know why – it was stupid, really. Just like a woman to lie about something like that if it got her what she wanted, but when he'd accused her of doing that, the hurt and outrage in her eyes was real. He never wanted to have her look at him that way again.

Which was why he was an idiot for talking about a dozen children. Hell, they couldn't even afford one –

not with the bank crawling down his neck. How was he supposed to break that to her? When was he supposed to tell her? Before the wedding or after?

The wedding that was due to take place in less than four weeks.

He'd better make a plan, and soon, for how to turn around this place and make it earn its keep. Otherwise he and his new bride would be shopping for both a new home and occupation on their honeymoon.

Autumn was right. They had to stop making love until they'd sorted out their problems and tied the knot. It wasn't fair to bring a new life into the world willy nilly without the kind of forethought that would keep a roof over its head. He'd go to his accountant in the morning and go over all the debts and income projections again. He'd figure out ways to cut costs and maximize his debt repayments.

He'd do whatever it took to start off his new life on a secure footing. His child deserved nothing less. His fiancée deserved far more.

Chapter Six

"Who the hell are you?"

Autumn nearly dropped her hoe before she whirled to face the unfamiliar woman marching up the garden path. She was taller than Autumn, with a strong jaw and no-nonsense, chin-length, dark bobbed hair. She clutched a folder in one hand and a purse in the other.

"Where's Ethan? What are you doing to my mother's garden?"

That explained it. Ethan's sister. What was her name? Claire – that was it.

"I'm waiting," Claire said.

Autumn moved to meet her, and held out a hand. "Hi, I'm Autumn."

Claire raised her eyebrows. "And?"

Autumn echoed her confused expression. "And?"

"So you're Autumn. Autumn who? What gives you the right to pulverize my mother's garlic bed?"

She glanced at the tidy rows she'd begun to take great pride in. She may have lied to Ethan about her green thumb, but she had found over the last few days that with a little common sense and a lot of help from the internet, she was able to sort the weeds from the useful plants and coax the garden back to life.

"Didn't Ethan tell you about me?"

Claire tapped a foot. "No, evidently he didn't. I take it you're Lacey's replacement?"

Lacey? A few things slid into place. She remembered Lacey from DelMonaco's her first night in town. How the brassy girl had stopped by the table with her obviously wealthy wanna-be cowboy husband-to-be. That's when Ethan announced their engagement. No – come to think of it, he hadn't – Rob had. Did Ethan want to keep it a secret? He sure had started drinking pretty heavily after that.

So had she, which led to their night of unbridled, unprotected passion, and the current predicament she found herself in. Five days had passed, and the thought of a baby growing inside her had hardly left her mind.

"I don't think I'm replacing anyone," she made herself say calmly. "I'm Ethan's fiancée."

"His what?" Claire straightened up. "Where is he?"

"Not here," Autumn managed to say before Claire pulled out a cell phone and punched in a bunch of numbers.

"Ethan? Dammit, don't you dare ignore me. You can't keep this ranch, not the way the debts are piling up. I want to sell and I want to sell now. You have something to say about that, you better come over here and tell me to my face." She ended the call and shoved the phone back in her purse. "Probably isn't even carrying the phone I gave him. He's totally hopeless. I hope you like city life, girl, because that's where my brother's going to end up just as soon as I pry him off this ranch. He's going to earn peanuts from the sale and he'll need a new job, quick. Not many of those around these parts, I can tell you that."

Autumn couldn't find her voice. The ranch was in debt? He was selling? Ethan hadn't mentioned a thing, and he thought they were getting married. When had he planned to tell his new bride about his financial troubles? After the wedding? When her money would be his?

Not that she had much, but what she had was hers – not his to use to solve his own problems.

"Just as I thought, he hasn't told you," Claire said, her expression hard. "Probably hasn't had time. You're not from around here, so who are you? Some fortune hunter? You saw the spread and thought you could cash in? You're a little too late for that. My momma already spent this fortune." She turned on her heel and paced away. "You might as well pack your bags and leave. My brother doesn't need any more heartache. He's had plenty already."

"Yeah, you'd know all about that, wouldn't you, Claire?"

Autumn turned to find Ethan descending the steps from the back porch. He must have pulled in at the front of the house where they couldn't see him. "Where have you been? I could use some help around the place, you know." He faced his sister.

"In Billings, making a living. We can't all throw good money after bad. Someone's got to be smarter than that."

"I can make a living right here; I just need a little help. There's nothing wrong with the ranch – the only problem is Momma's debts." He ran a hand through his hair and glanced at Autumn. "Hell, Claire. You had to do it this way?"

Claire put her hands on her hips and leaned closer to him. "She said she's your fiancée. Your fiancée! When were you going to tell me, Ethan? After the wedding? And you obviously didn't tell her about your money problems. That's not right! None of this is – where did you even meet her?"

Autumn felt her face burning and even Ethan looked flushed. "That's none of your business. What are you here for, anyway?" He crossed his arms.

"This ranch is half mine. Did you forget that?" Claire shook her head at him and the severe edges of her bob brushed her chin. "It's time to sell. Let's get what we can from it and move on. I've mocked up a listing. Look it over and see if I got it all right." She shoved the folder into his hands.

"And what about me, huh, Claire? It's all right for me to be an employee all my life?" He kicked a watering can across the garden. "I've worked this ranch since I could walk."

"You can do something else."

"I don't want to do something else."

Claire clenched her fists. "Then buy me out. This dream is over, Ethan. The ranch is done."

"Claire!"

But she'd already stormed off across the yard. In a moment she was out of sight around the corner of the bunkhouse and they heard an engine start up.

Ethan turned slowly around. "I'm sorry. Claire's right; I should have told you. I just didn't expect…"

"How bad is it?" She didn't know why she was asking. She'd be gone in a week or two, back to her old life and old job. She hoped, anyway. This man was nothing to her. So what if he lied? The cold burn of fire in her gut told her it mattered a lot, but she forced that thought away. All men were liars. She'd known that since she was nine and watched her mother – her fun-loving, wonderful, warm mother turn overnight into an icy automaton, too busy and too hurt to open her heart to anyone – even her own daughters. She remembered the pain of that first year after he'd left. Her attempts to make her mother happy again.

Her failures.

"Bad. My mother," he waved the folder in dismissal. "I loved her, but she didn't belong on a ranch. She wanted to travel, live the high life. My Dad let her spend all he had, and then let her spend a whole lot more he didn't have."

A familiar tension twisted in her stomach as she remembered taking on the task of managing her family's budget. Always good with numbers, and a better cook than Lily, first she took over the grocery shopping and meal preparation, then the rest of the bills as Teresa finished med school and began work. Adding up numbers that didn't add up over and over again. Trying to make too little money stretch too far. Finding fifty ways to prepare beans and rice. "And just exactly when did you plan to say something – on our wedding night?"

The fury in her words made him flinch and she barely understood her own anger. After all, she was lying to him as much as he'd been lying to her, so why did it hurt so bad to find out that her cowboy groom was as big a jerk as her father?

Because her father hadn't just broken her mother's heart when he left; he'd broken hers, too. How many nights had she lain awake as a girl wondering what she'd done to drive him away. Was it the way she looked? The way she cried sometimes when she got hurt? The way she got a bad grade in spelling? For nine years he'd been a mainstay in her life – at the breakfast table in the morning, reading the newspaper when he got home at night, tucking her into bed with a tousle of her hair and a kiss on the forehead. Telling her he loved her.

But he didn't. One day he was there. The next he was gone. And her mother might as well have gone, too. Even Lily changed. Suddenly mad all the time, ordering her around, pinching her when she made mistakes. "The house has to be clean. Hurry up, the dishes need to be done before she gets home. Clean up your toys, you want Mom to leave, too?"

"You have every right to be mad. I didn't…" He hesitated. Making up more lies? "Listen, Autumn – I had no idea this would work." He waved a hand to include the two of them. "I thought you'd leave as soon as you got to know me and saw what life out here looks like. You're a city girl – why would you want to marry me and live like this? Even without the debt, it's not like we're ever going to be rich. You could have any guy. Why would you stay here with me?"

His question struck her squarely in the gut. Why would she stay with him? Was it possible this handsome, self-confident cowboy had doubts of his own?

Maybe he did, she conceded, his explanations finally catching up with her. Sounds like his childhood wasn't all roses and sunshine, either.

Well, she wasn't going to stay, was she? Except she wanted to with every fiber of her being. She knew that a life with Ethan meant hard work and the ups and downs of being dependent on your own two hands to make a living, but she also knew it would never be boring and that the challenges would most likely bring them together in a way city living never could. And Ethan…over the last few days he'd driven her all over the ranch, showing her the land he loved and the cattle herds he depended on to make his living. He talked about how he was considering raising buffalo, and he told her stories about growing up here and learning to ride. The funniest stories, however, were the ones that included Rob, Cab and Jamie. She couldn't believe how much trouble they'd found over the years, or the way they tormented each other with practical jokes. It was amazing they'd never landed in jail – and even more amazing that Cab grew up to be a sheriff.

Ethan was so patient around the animals, and so dedicated to running the ranch right. After dinner each night he spent time in the tiny office off his bedroom updating the ranch's accounts. She had a feeling he kept track of his money down to the penny. Now she knew why.

But it was the evenings she loved the most. After he'd done his books and she'd downloaded her photographs and written her notes, they'd meet again on the back porch to hold hands, talk and swing. They'd decided heavy petting was allowed, which often turned into a romp on top of the covers on Ethan's bed. As much as they did their best to satisfy each other without actually making love, Autumn didn't think she could ever be satisfied until she had him again – body and soul. She wanted to stay here with Ethan more than anything else in the world. She wanted to be his wife.

"Yeah, that's what I thought," Ethan said gruffly when she hesitated too long. "You don't. And Claire's right – I probably have to sell. Might as well get it all over with. I'll take you to the airport in the morning."

With that he strode to the back door and let it shut behind him with a bang. Alone in the garden, Autumn looked at the neat rows of plants reaching for the sun. She surveyed the fields that ran to far off mountains.

She didn't want to go.

The large house across the yard caught her attention and once again she thought it was a shame no one lived in it. It was a beautiful log home, with wide decks and a stunning view of the mountains. If she was on vacation she'd spend a mint to rent one of those rooms.

Autumn's heart skipped a beat, recalling a bunch of brochures Becka brought home from a travel agent's office back in New York when she was trying to learn all she could about her prospective cowboy husband. They were advertisements for guest ranches and together she and Becka had laughed about the rustic accommodations and tourists dressed up like cowboys in shiny new boots.

A guest ranch – that was the answer to Ethan's problems.

And she could help.

Chapter Seven

Ethan leaned on the rails surrounding the north pen and watched Jamie work with a black Appaloosa, trying to figure out where everything had gone to hell. He'd tried to stay indoors, but when Autumn didn't follow him into the kitchen, he knew he'd been right. She was leaving him. He felt sick to his stomach and he wasn't sure he would be able to stand if the rough wooden railings weren't holding him up. Autumn was probably packing her bags by now and he had plenty of chores to do – especially if he was going to blow tomorrow morning hauling her to the airport. So why was he standing here wasting time, feeling like he'd been sucker-punched?

He knew from the day Autumn arrived he'd be sending her back home. This was all a practical joke, after all. Shit, he couldn't believe how out of control it had all gotten. Rob was to blame for this and he'd sure pay him back good.

Except that's what started all of this, wasn't it? Payback?

No – it began earlier than that. With his parents' death. If it weren't for the accident they'd be here now and his father would be overseeing the ranch. Maybe he'd have confessed his debts and the trouble they were in and together they could have reined in his mother's spending and turned things around.

But as he flipped through his memories, he had to admit his family was in trouble long before the car crash. Claire and his mother had been fighting for years. Claire was a difficult teenager. As soon as she got a figure and discovered boys, life in the Cruz family household went to the dogs.

He couldn't remember how many mornings he'd showed up for breakfast after completing his chores to find his mother and sister screaming in the kitchen, or slamming their respective bedroom doors. Claire was wild, used to getting her own way, with just as big a desire as his mother to be the center of attention.

Ethan stiffened. Was that true? Did his mother want attention?

He thought back to the last few years of her life. He hadn't paid much attention to the clothing, jewelry and home decorating which seemed the foundation of his mother's daily rounds. He was too busy working for his Dad, going to school and competing in the local rodeos when he could. He was saving money for a car, and looking forward to the day he graduated and put school behind him for good. No university for him, thank you very much. He'd leave that nightmare to Claire.

Although, in her younger years Claire had no more desire than he did to attend college. She was the best female rider this side of...well...anywhere. A natural on a horse and completely fearless. No one could touch her – not even Jamie when she was really on fire. She'd spent every spare minute with the horses, in the training corrals or out on the range riding for hours, coming home far after dinner time, sometimes far after dark. The fights between Claire and their parents got so bad that Ethan learned to pack himself enough food he could go straight to school from his chores in his morning and straight back to his chores after school without ever setting foot in the war zone of the Cruz kitchen. He spent his afternoons working any job his father set him, but whenever he could get away, he'd make his way to this pen and watch Mack MacKenzie work with the horses.

Mack had lived and worked on the ranch since Ethan was ten and felt like one of the family. He was a cowboy through and through, with a swagger to his step, a joke at the ready, and a laugh that boomed out over the yard and made everyone in earshot turn to look. He seemed larger than life – a heck of a lot more fun than his quiet father, who only opened his mouth to issue orders, or so it seemed to him at the time.

His mother would come out of the Big House sometimes to bring him a glass of lemonade, and always brought one for Mack, too. He knew she did it for an excuse to step outside and get away from the cooking and cleaning that took up her days whenever she was home. He didn't blame her – how any woman could stand inside work when the sun was blazing away in the wide Montana sky he never could fathom. He figured her frequent trips abroad were an antidote to the boredom of being a rancher's wife.

Claire spent plenty of time at this corral, too, of course. Mack actually let her into the pen when he was working with new horses. For someone who spent half her day screaming, she had a way about her when animals were present.

Ethan smiled at the memory, then frowned as he turned to look at the Big House and saw Autumn striding purposefully up the walk to the front door. With her damn camera in her hand.

What the hell?

Jamie turned, too. "Hey Ethan. How's it going with your new bride? Surprised to see you haven't sent her packing yet." He cocked his head as he watched her turn the handle on the front door to the Big House and hesitate, as if surprised to find it unlocked. She stepped inside.

Why hadn't he sent her packing? Because he thought she was different than all the other women in his life? Because he thought maybe she might have more sense, or less avarice, or the ability to string a couple of sentences together in a row without lying? Had he lost her because of the ranch's debts, or because he hadn't told her about them sooner?

"I gotta go," he said.

"Hey, take it easy on her," Jamie said, and Ethan looked back at the wiry man who'd taken Mack's job when the other man left the ranch. "She's probably just curious, that's all. She only knows as much of your history as you've told her."

"What the hell do you care?"

Jamie shook his head and snorted at his hostility. "She's a sight better than Lacey – any fool can see that, even at a distance. She's not your mother or your sister. She's a girl who came out here because she wants to live on a ranch with a cowboy for a husband. You need a woman around, so why don't you give her half a chance before you go driving her away? Maybe she'll surprise you."

Ethan followed his gaze to the Big House, where Autumn was just visible in the living room windows. "Too late – I've already driven her away."

"You sure about that? She doesn't look like she's going anywhere."

Ethan shrugged, squashing the tendril of hope Jamie's words stirred within him. Autumn hadn't brought much with her to Montana. She was probably already packed and bored and just needed something to fill the rest of the day.

Jamie turned back to the horse and Ethan strode for the Big House, his friend's words echoing in his ears. Maybe she wasn't leaving. After all, she might be carrying his child.

He waved off the thought. What were the chances of that?

You made love to her without protection – the chances might be better than you think.

Maybe that's why she was walking through the Big House – to estimate how much they could earn from the sale of the ranch. Maybe she intended to file for child support and wanted to be able to tell the court exactly how much he was worth. His blood began to boil. That's all he needed – another creditor to drive him under. If she thought he would sell just to support her and the baby…

Oh, hell. What was he thinking? Of course he'd do whatever it took support his wife and child. And if she refused to marry him now, he'd still do what he had to in order to keep a roof over his baby's head and food on the table. He might pay for the rest of his life for that one, thoughtless night of passion, but he'd make damn sure his kid didn't pay for it. That wasn't fair.

What if Autumn took the baby back to New York? Could he stand that? A city was no place to raise a child – not by his way of thinking anyway. Kids needed room to run, horses to ride, trouble to get into – good, clean, safe trouble. He blew out a breath as his thoughts circled around again. He needed to think of some way to keep this ranch, to force Autumn to stay and marry him, and to raise his child here. Right here.

Because that would be his definition of paradise, wouldn't it? Not just any ranch – this one. Not just any wife – Autumn. And not just any child – but theirs, the first of many more to come.

Autumn was in the Big House and he'd better get in there, too, and start explaining things to her. Claire was right; the sale would clear all the family's debts and leave a little for starting over, but not enough to buy another ranch. Barely enough to buy a house in town.

Then what would he do? Put on a suit and tie and go to work for the bank? Not likely they'd have him, with his high school diploma and work-scarred hands.

What a hell of a mess.

Chapter Eight

Autumn wasn't sure what she'd been expecting when she opened the door to the Big House. Cobwebs, maybe. Dust as thick as a carpet over everything.

Though the house had a whiff of the mustiness she expected from a home that hadn't been lived in for months, it was otherwise immaculate. The electricity was on, she discovered when she flicked a switch in the entryway. She walked into a foyer the size of her New York apartment, that led straight into a great room whose ceiling soared two stories above. A massive staircase to her left led to a balcony from which she assumed one reached the bedrooms. The living room windows overlooked the ranch buildings in the foreground and on to a sweeping view of the Beartooth Mountains that took her breath away.

A counter separated the fully-equipped restaurant quality kitchen from the living room. The cook would never feel cut off from the action, especially not with the sink and oven positioned so she could face the living room and the view while making use of them. Her fingers itched to get to work. What feasts she could prepare here, and how lovely a setting in which to do so. She pictured guests taking their ease in the comfortable chairs and sofas by the floor-to-ceiling windows, resting their tired limbs after a day of trail riding and "helping" the ranch hands with their chores.

She'd circulate with trays of appetizers and cold drinks, making sure everyone felt right at home, while a roast or hearty stew sent tantalizing aromatic hints of the meal to come. A rustic plank table and chairs already sat in one corner of the huge living room. She counted 18 places and wondered how Ethan's small family had kept from feeling overwhelmed at such a large table. Maybe the ranch hands lived on the property back in those days, and ate with them, or maybe they had frequently had company.

The house was beautiful and her heart ached at the thought of it standing empty for so many months. Ethan's grief must have consumed him if he couldn't bear to live here after his parent's deaths. Who took care of it now? she wondered. Claire? Somehow she didn't think so. She repressed an urge to shiver. The woman's anger at finding her on the property had been palpable, but she had the feeling Claire's anger went a lot deeper than being last to hear about Ethan's engagement. She'd stumbled into a family with issues, that was for sure.

After examining the kitchen more closely – a six burner range, professional grade pots and pans that gleamed with care, a refrigerator twice the size of the one in her apartment, and every gadget and gizmo a chef could want – she took photographs of the main floor from every angle. She was halfway up the stairs to the balcony when the sound of the front door opening halted her in her tracks.

Ethan stepped into view, cocking his hat back the better to look at her. "One point two million," he said.

"I beg your pardon?" Her heart was in her throat, but not at being found trespassing. Ethan was so handsome in his jeans, work shirt, and cowboy hat, she couldn't tear her gaze from his face. How could she ever leave this man?

"The ranch. It's worth about one million, two hundred thousand dollars."

Her mouth dropped open. That was a chunk of change.

"Don't get too excited; my mother had the uncanny ability to spend more money in a year than most municipalities." He started up the stairs. "Add in an equally uncanny ability to find doomed investments and the money from the sale of the ranch will barely cover the debts she left." He stopped on the tread beneath hers. She found his proximity made it hard to breathe. Neither could she look away from him. He held her gaze and leaned closer. "Whatever is left, I have to split with Claire. I'll be lucky to be able to put a roof over my head. Not the best situation to bring a wife, and maybe a child, into."

"We'll manage," she heard herself say. This close to him she couldn't think straight. She found his eyes mesmerizing, the line of his jaw fascinating, and had to grip the banister to keep from running her own mouth along his collar bone to the hollow at the base of his throat. No one was around, and she couldn't imagine they'd be interrupted. She'd bet those bedrooms would be furnished with the finest of beds, and if they couldn't make it that far, the plush carpeting on these stairs would just have to do.

She leaned toward him, her lips parting.

Their kiss was as sweet as anything she'd known. He was hesitant at first, but when she put a hand on his chest, he groaned and swept her into his arms. She dropped the camera and clung to him, her hunger for his touch overriding her moment's fear they'd overbalance and fall together down the stairs. She snaked her arms around his neck and kissed him with a passion that flared from tinder to full-on flame.

When his hand slid down the curve of her back to cup her bottom, Autumn gasped, then kissed him harder. Suddenly she couldn't stand the layers of clothing between them. She wriggled in his arms until she could reach the buttons of his shirt. She made short work of them and was just reaching for her own when Ethan's hand covered hers at the top of her neckline and he pulled apart her dress with a single tug. Buttons scattered and another rough tug took care of her bra – a front clasped one, thank goodness – releasing her breasts to his view. Ethan pulled back for a single moment, looked her over, then pushed her down to a sitting position, leaned her back against the stair treads, and bent to take one nipple into his mouth.

Autumn writhed beneath him, glorying in the touch of his mouth, his tongue on her flesh. As he swept from one breast to the other and back again, the sensation swirled over her, through her and heated her to the core. She knocked off his hat and fisted her hands in his thick hair, moaning again as he dipped lower, lower, and nuzzled her sensitive core.

"Ethan," she gasped, then arched her back as his tongue took her even higher.

Moments later he was back in her arms, covering her body with his, as naked as she'd somehow become.

"Autumn." Her name was a question and she understood him completely. Was she sure she wanted this?

"Protection?" she gasped and he hesitated a fraction of a second.

"Wait," he said and kissed her once more, a rough scrape of his mouth against hers. Then he was gone and she shivered in his absence. Before she could question it, he was back, a condom in hand. "My old stash," he whispered. He had it on in an instant, then touched her chin, capturing her gaze once more. "Do you trust me?"

She nodded. Leaning forward he kissed her forehead, each of her eyes, her nose and then her mouth, covering her once more with his own lean, hard body.

She braced herself for his thrust, but opened her eyes again when he gently turned her in his arms. He guided her forearms to one stair tread, her knees to a lower one, framing her body with his own.

"Is this all right?" he breathed into her ear. He shifted forward, and his hardness pressed against her core, igniting an inner fire so bright it was all she could do not to press back against him and take him inside with one hard thrust.

"Autumn?"

"Yes," she said, her voice so strained it was barely recognizable. "Yes. Please."

She'd barely finished speaking when he pushed inside her. She cried out and he grunted, pulling out and pressing in again. He braced himself with a single hand on the stairs, using the other to cup her breasts. The sensation of him entering from behind her was breathtaking, but when he slid that hand down between her legs, the feeling was beyond any words.

Autumn bucked against him, the rhythm of his thrusts stoking the fire within her to new heights. She twisted her head to kiss him, to breathe raggedly into his ear, and when she nipped his earlobe, he redoubled his efforts, causing her to moan aloud.

Ethan's pace quickened, her breasts swung in their own parallel rhythm, her sensitive nipples tantalized by the friction of the silky carpet against their tips. She arched her hips and pressed back into him, not able to get enough, unable to quench the thirst her body had developed for his touch.

Ethan grunted again, low and guttural, and Autumn clung to him, swept over the edge by want and need and desire. Ecstasy exploded within her, tossing her on wave after wave of sensation until she cried out again, bucking up against his hips, pressing her breasts down against the soft tread, closing her eyes in utter abandon to this lovemaking the likes of which she'd never known.

They collapsed together, full length on the stairs, Autumn taking his weight gladly until lack of oxygen made her wiggle and he pushed himself up on his elbows. She sighed with disappointment when he pulled out, and turned to snuggle in the curve of his shoulder as he lay beside her, still breathing hard.

"Woman, you'll be the death of me if you keep up like that," he said.

His exaggerated western drawl made her smile and she kissed the underside of his chin. "Can we do it again?"

He laughed aloud, and traced the length of her arm with one finger. "Any time." He dropped a kiss on her cheek. "Any time at all." Then he sobered. "But not too much longer on these stairs, I guess. Not if Claire has her way. I know I could pay off our debts over time, but buying out her half of the ranch – that's just impossible. I don't know what I'm going to do without this place."

"What if you didn't have to sell," Autumn said, pulling back to see his face better. "What if you could keep the ranch and still buy her out?"

"What do you have in mind?" He sat up, placed his hat back on top of his head and began to dress.

She bit her lip. She only had the barest kernel of a plan. "Give me 24 hours, okay? I have an idea but I need more time to think it through. Tomorrow at dinner I'll make a presentation."

"A presentation? Like with a slideshow?" He laughed, and his smile warmed her heart.

She laughed with him. "Sure – I'll do a Powerpoint presentation. I'll lay everything out. Except…"

"Except what?"

"I don't really know the numbers – what you bring in now, what your costs are. You've only known me a week, so I'll understand if you don't want to show me the books."

Ethan glanced back up the stairs. "I'd say I know you better than I should at this point. And you are going to be my wife. And you might be carrying my child. If you want to look at the books, have at it. You know anything about numbers?"

Autumn picked up her camera and nodded. Boy, did she.

Chapter Nine

When Ethan returned from his afternoon chores, the smell of dinner made him want to skip his shower and head straight for the kitchen table, but Autumn shooed him along with a bright smile. "Fifteen minutes until the potatoes are done."

Ten minutes later found him showered, changed and shaved, but he could still hear Autumn moving around the kitchen, so he let himself into the tiny room off of his bedroom he had converted into his office to pull out the ledgers he used to keep his accounts.

Matt Underwood, his accountant, swore at him every quarter when he brought in the dusty, old books to be photocopied by his secretary.

"Hell's bells, Ethan – you're the only holdout left in three counties. You own a laptop, so buy some software and get with the new century, would you? I'll even set up the accounting program for you. You can punch in a few numbers, click your mouse and send in everything I need without leaving the ranch."

He let Matt rant on, but it never made a difference. He wasn't interested in fancy gadgets or pecking away at a machine. He hated the cell phone Claire had given him and his laptop sat untouched on his desk. The ledgers were good enough for five generations of Cruz's; they were good enough for him.

But when he entered his study, it wasn't account books that caught his eye. It was the collage of photographs covering a large portion of the windowless wall to the right of his desk. He saw it every time he entered the office, but it had been months since he really took it in. It had become as much a part of the tiny room as his desk and the ledger books.

Lacey made the collage after his parents' accident, when he'd moved into the bunkhouse, but before he confessed the extent of the financial trouble he was in and she'd left him for good. One day, she asked him to take her to a home and garden show in Billings, and he'd begged off, saying he needed to work on his accounts. He had just learned the extent of his debts and was still reeling from his parents' death and he couldn't stand to spend the day listening to Lacey make lists of all the things she wanted to buy, and he could no longer afford.

True to his word, he'd spent the day holed up in his study, going over and over the accounts. That evening, he'd driven to her house to find she wasn't home. She didn't answer her cell phone, either. Typical Lacey behavior when she was mad about something. Unfortunately, he knew her other typical behaviors – getting drunk and flirting with other men. After spending half the night looking for her in every bar and restaurant within 50 miles of town and coming up empty, he'd returned to the bunkhouse to find a trail of roses leading back to this tiny room.

The photos she'd glued to the wall showed Lacey in every season, indoors and outdoors, smiling and pouting, in various states of dress and undress. In the very center she'd placed a photo he'd taken of her with her own camera one morning after they'd shared a bed. Only partially wrapped in a comforter, the early spring sunshine streaming in his bedroom window and cascading over her ripe body, the photo was as provocative as anything in a skin magazine. Even now it reminded him he was a man looking at a beautiful, naked woman.

He had the same thought he'd had every night this week when he entered the room to update his books. He'd better get rid of this before Autumn saw it. So far he hadn't found the time to get it done and he wouldn't be able to do it now, either. It was going to take time to scrape the pictures off the wall, especially since he had no idea how Lacey had attached them. Some sort of fancy craft store glue and then a layer of varnish over the whole damn thing. Autumn hollered from the kitchen to say that dinner was ready. Tonight, when she was getting ready for bed, he'd scrape them from the wall into a bag and hide them, and tomorrow when he was out working on the range, he'd light a little fire and burn them all.

Autumn jotted down another item on her shopping list. She'd ask Ethan if she could borrow the truck tomorrow. She planned to start the day by going over the ranch's accounts and doing some research. Then she'd head to town, shop, and pop into his accountant's office to get answers to any questions she might have. Then it would be back to the ranch to do a bit of work on the garden and prepare her presentation. She knew the guest ranch idea wouldn't solve every problem right away, but she thought they might be able to pull it off. She opened the oven door and pulled out the stew pot, carried it over to the table and placed it on a square oven mitt she'd pressed into service as a trivet. Ethan might be able to pull it off, that is. She wouldn't be here by then, of course.

Suddenly chilled, she crossed her arms and hugged them to her chest. Their passionate lovemaking and the afternoon spent gardening and cooking had driven all thought of her return to New York right out of her mind. She'd been thinking about the number of bedrooms in the Big House; how many guests they could hold and how to increase that number without building a costly addition. She was as adept with numbers as she was in the kitchen, and the hours had passed quickly and happily, but now that reality had burst her bubble she realized more than ever she didn't want to return to city life.

The light from the workaday kitchen fixture made the diamond ring on her finger sparkle. Maybe the guest ranch idea could solve two problems in one fell swoop. Maybe it could save the ranch and provide her with a new career. If she was contributing as much to the bottom line as Ethan was, wouldn't that count? Her mother and sister couldn't gainsay that idea, could they?

Maybe it was time she stopped caring so much what they thought, anyway. No other man made her feel like Ethan did. No man had ever made her want to give up her independence and settle down. The idea of running a guest ranch, and better yet – cooking for a crowd every night, a crowd that someday would include her own children – made her heart lift with excitement. Surely that beat writing silly columns for a ladies' magazine any day.

Didn't it?

Glancing down at her ring again, she squared her shoulders. Why not grasp at the chance life was giving her. A handsome, caring fiancé who loved children. A chance to start a family and a new, exciting career. In less than a month she could have everything she ever wanted.

When Ethan walked into the room it was all she could do not to throw herself into his arms.

"Yes!" she said.

He stopped, one hand on the back of his chair, and cocked his head. "Yes?"

She nodded. "Yes. I want to marry you. Absolutely yes."

And when the smile broke across his handsome face and he came to take her in his arms, she thought she'd found heaven right here on earth.

Chapter Ten

It was noon by the time Autumn reached Matt Underwood's office. When she'd headed toward Ethan's office earlier, he'd quickly forestalled her and went to fetch his accounting information himself. She'd nearly cried when Ethan dumped the stack of leather-covered old-fashioned ledger books on the kitchen table. She'd expected him to hand her a laptop with QuickAccounts or a similar program booted up and ready to access. What should have taken minutes ended up taking hours and she still didn't have a complete handle on the Cruz operation.

A call to Matt's office had gotten her commiseration and an invitation to come right in to get help. Apparently, Ethan had called earlier, letting Matt know who she was and why she was looking over the account books. As soon as Matt found out she was computer literate he begged her to use any and all influence she had on Ethan to get him online, as well.

Matt turned out to be in his mid-thirties, a trim man with a sharp face and horn-rimmed glasses. He listened carefully while she outlined her idea to turn the Big House into guest accommodations and offer trail rides, a cowboy experience, and trips into Billings for shopping and cultural events.

"It might work," Matt said finally. "But you've got several obstacles, not the least of which is Ethan's sister, Claire. You do know she wants to sell the ranch and pocket her half of the proceeds, right?"

"I know. What would it take to buy her out?"

It took nearly an hour for Matt to explain the exact state of affairs at the ranch. On the one hand, very few changes needed to be made to any of the existing structures to accommodate a fair number of guests. They would need a liquor license if they wanted to serve alcohol with dinner, and Autumn would need to take a food safety course. They might need extra hands to help with the trail rides; she knew very little about the men who worked with Ethan and their qualifications to interact with paying guests. Advertising would cost money and it would take time to drum up the interest and repeat customers that were the bread and butter of any guesthouse type arrangement.

Securing a loan to buy out Claire would be the toughest part of the battle. Autumn wished she had more to offer on that part of the bargain. Still, Matt thought two things might help. The first, oddly enough, was their marriage. He said bankers were old-fashioned in Montana, and they'd look favorably on a man who clearly planned to settle down and make a go of his spread. He also knew of a man interested in purchasing some land in the area. If Ethan could be persuaded to sell 100 acres on the riverfront, the profits would help swing them a second mortgage on the rest of the property. It might take a week or two for the buyer to get things together, but Claire would get paid and they'd have enough cash left over to advertise, buy some more riding horses, and get their guest ranch up and running.

As she stood up to shake Matt's hand, her stomach rumbled, reminding her she hadn't even eaten breakfast. She'd joined Ethan in his bed the previous night not long after dinner, and even though they'd been together more than once before falling asleep, both woke with an ardor that required quenching before any of the day's work could begin.

She'd crammed half a loaf of French bread and an apple into Ethan's hands as he ran out the door to meet Jamie in the south pasture. She hoped he wouldn't be too upset at her absence from home at lunch time, but she still needed to do her shopping before she headed back to the ranch.

"Hungry?" Matt said. "I'm heading over to Linda's Diner for a bite. Want to join me?"

"Sure." Autumn checked her watch. "Are they fairly quick? I've still got a lot to do today."

"We'll have you in and out of there in a jiffy. I know all the waitresses – I'll tell them you're in a hurry."

They crossed the road to a small restaurant sandwiched between the post office and a barber shop. Matt chose a table by the window and waved over a blonde waitress wearing a short-sleeved white shirt, black skirt, and a red apron with the Linda's Diner logo stitched in white.

"Hi Matt, want the usual?"

"Yep. Tracey, this is Autumn Leeds. She's in a bit of a rush today, so I promised lunch wouldn't take too long."

"No problem! What can I get you, Autumn?"

Autumn liked the young woman's cheerful smile. "What's the usual?"

"BLT, fries, and a chocolate milkshake."

"Sounds perfect. I'll have one, too."

"Coming right up. Cook's probably got yours halfway done already, Matt."

Tracey swung away, stopping at the next table to drop off a bill, before heading toward the counter that ran the length of one side of the building. She relayed the order to an older woman with graying hair pulled into a high bun.

"Is that Linda?"

Matt looked over his shoulder and laughed. "Naw, that's Stephanie Lakins. Linda was her great grandma. It's kind of a family business."

"I guess so." She returned Matt's smile. "What made you pick accounting?" She settled back in her chair, confident that lunch would be tasty and the company enjoyable enough to pass the time.

As the door opened with a chime of bells, however, her feeling of contentment fell away in an instant. She recognized that brassy blonde hair, stiletto heels, and much too short skirt. Lacey Taylor, Ethan's ex-fiancee. Was it too late to hide?

Lacey spotted her, narrowed her eyes, and dragged Carl with her over to stand before Autumn.

Yes, it was.

"Well, good morning – look what we have here!" she trilled, looking from Autumn to Matt and back again. "Are you negotiating your pre-nup with Ethan's accountant, or moving on to greener pastures?"

Carl looked distinctly uncomfortable and Autumn wondered why he didn't say anything. Probably out of fear Lacey would leave him like she left Ethan. Men seemed infinitely able to overlook a woman's bitchiness if her breasts were perky and her feet stuffed into a pair of high heels.

"None of your business, Lacey," Matt said. "You just run along and play."

Autumn bit her lip to keep from laughing at Lacey's expression. Clearly, she wasn't used to being brushed aside so easily. She bent down, dangling her ample breasts directly in Matt's line of sight. The accountant raised an eyebrow. "I'm just looking out for Ethan, honey. Who is this woman, anyway? She appears out of nowhere, suddenly she's engaged to him and now she's having lunch with his accountant? You better believe I'm going to tell him I saw the two of you together. If you think you can mess with my man, you're highly mistaken." She finished by narrowing her eyes at Autumn.

"Your man?" Carl and Matt chimed together. Autumn was too busy letting her jaw drop to the ground to say anything.

"Oh...you know what I mean," Lacey said, her color heightening. "I may not want to marry Ethan Cruz, but that doesn't mean I don't have his best interests at heart. I don't want to see him taken to the cleaners by some New York City call girl."

"Seriously?" Autumn squeaked. "Did you just call me a hooker?" She stood up, but so did Matt. He put a hand on her arm and stepped between her and Lacey.

"Carl, if I were you I'd get Lacey out of here before she makes a complete ass out of herself. People are watching."

Carl put an arm around Lacey and tugged her toward the door. "Come on, Sugar, let's try the Soup n' Salad today; I'm not in the mood for diner food."

"I'm not done here!" Lacey shrugged him off and turned on Autumn. "You know Ethan's broke, don't you? You know he has to sell the ranch?" She took Autumn's speechlessness as a negative. "See, Carl – he's doing it again! Honey, he's lying to you just like he did to me. Let me guess – first he wined and dined you, made you feel all quivery with those baby blue eyes, put his diamond ring on your finger...and didn't even bother to let you know he's up to his eyeballs in debt. Am I right or am I right?" She leaned closer. "That's exactly what he did to me. I had to learn about his money problems from Claire – his sister. Have you met his sister?"

Autumn nodded.

"Good. I hope she told you the ranch is for sale."

Carl tugged on Lacey's arm. "Sugar, that's enough. Let's go."

"We're going to buy it, you know. Me and Carl. Isn't that right, Carl?"

Carl closed his eyes and for a split second Autumn almost felt sorry for the man. Almost. "Honey, I thought we decided to keep that a secret."

"You decided that. I want Ethan and his new fiancée to know exactly who's buying their property. Ethan's land is next to Carl's, you know. When we merge them we'll have the biggest spread in four counties. If Ethan's looking for work, maybe we'll hire him. Maybe."

"Lacey, that's enough. Out the door – now."

Autumn blinked when Carl nearly picked Lacey up and shoved her bodily out the front door. Her mind spun with the information she'd just learned. "Is she for real?" She'd better let Ethan know Lacey's plans as soon as possible, although she didn't relish the idea. Ethan was going to blow his top.

"Oh, Lacey's always been like that, but I didn't think Carl would be such an idiot," Matt said. "He's already an outsider in this town, coming here and building his McMansion on the old Frommer ranch. If he takes the Cruz ranch..." He shook his head. "He'll be mighty unpopular."

"I'm not sure he cares about being popular." She pushed a lock of hair behind her ear. "He just cares about Lacey. I think Lacey still cares about Ethan, though. At least she doesn't want him to move on."

"She's out for vengeance, I'd say." She appreciated the calm confidence of this man. He was going to make someone a good husband someday, if he wasn't already married. "And she'll do whatever it takes to get it. Your sudden appearance in town has raised questions, you know. You and Ethan might want to tell your story to a few of the local gossips before someone else starts a story for you, if you know what I mean."

"Thanks for the advice," she said slowly. What did Matt think of her relationship with Ethan? What would everyone think if they knew the truth of why she'd come here? She needed to cut her ties with the magazine, get her ducks in order and put her relationship with Ethan on solid ground – fast – before someone discovered the truth and broadcast it. All of this was so crazy – so backwards! First she'd agreed to marriage – well, she'd fake-agreed to it; then she'd gotten pregnant – maybe; and now she was falling in love with her intended.

Wait.

What?

Did she love Ethan?

Yes, she did.

How could she – she'd barely known him a week.

Yet his every touch took her breath away, the life he led called to her like nothing else ever had. She wanted what this marriage would bring her – a husband, a family, a career, even a community. She would have a place in all of it that was just for her.

She thought about Ethan's concern for her wellbeing since she'd arrived, the work ethic that had him racing out to the fields before dawn to meet his crew and get to his chores, the loyalty to ranch, family and hired help that made him want to turn things around for the benefit of all of them. And the way he made love to her...

Yes, she loved Ethan Cruz.

But did he love her back?

She thought so. She'd just have to stick around long enough to find out. And that meant presenting her plan to save the ranch to Ethan before Claire got too caught up in the idea of selling it to Lacey. Now that she had all the information she needed, she'd get her shopping done fast and head right home. Would Ethan agree her idea was a good one?

Would it work?

When Ethan said good-bye to Jamie and headed home to the bunkhouse, he found pizza cooking in the oven – homemade, by the looks of things – but Autumn nowhere to be found. Ten minutes remained on the timer, and he hoped he could get a shower in before they sat down to eat.

"Autumn?"

As he moved down the hall, he heard the clack of fingernails on a keyboard. Was she still working on that proposal?

"Autumn? You in there?"

"Yep! Just finishing up." He heard a rustle of paper and the rattling sound of an office chair being pushed away from a desk.

"Do I have time for a shower?" He poked his head around the door and was unexpectedly met by a kiss.

"Sure, if you're fast. Don't be too long, though – we really need to talk about my plan." She returned to the small corner desk and began to type again.

"I can be fast." He waited a beat for her to laugh, but she was already engrossed in the spreadsheet on her laptop again. She really must be into this idea of hers, whatever it was. He hoped she wasn't getting her hopes up too high that they could keep the ranch. Oh, who was he kidding – his hopes were high and he didn't have the slightest idea how to manage it. Sighing, he headed for their bedroom and began to strip down.

The hot water sluiced away all the dust and aches of eleven hours spent out of doors doing physical work. It had been the kind of day he liked best. Work to do and typical ranch problems to solve, but nothing insurmountable – and no new bills. Jamie was always a good companion. He knew when to talk and when to keep quiet, and he always pulled his own weight.

He wished he could offer him the guarantee of a stable income. It weighed on him that if he didn't figure out something quick, Jamie would be one of the first to suffer. Of course a horseman like him could find work on just about any ranch. Still, he treated Jamie like family – always had – and he knew that counted a lot with a man.

Had Autumn found a way to buy out his sister? It would be a miracle, and he could use one of those right about now.

Five minutes later he was sitting at the kitchen table, biting off the triangular end of a slice of the most delicious pizza he'd ever had. Autumn sat across from him, her hands held stiffly in her lap. Was she nervous? Maybe he shouldn't have started eating yet. He dropped the slice back on his plate, wiped his hands and took a drink of milk.

"Sorry. I couldn't help myself – the pizza smells great. Tastes great, too."

She smiled a little. "I have some bad news and some good news. I'm going to tell you the bad news first. Please don't get upset."

Crud. That didn't sound good. "Okay – shoot."

She took a deep breath. "Lacey and Carl want to buy the ranch. They've already talked to Claire about it. Ethan, you promised!"

He surged out of his chair so fast it tipped over. "They what? Uh-uh, no way. They'll have to pry the deed out of my dead, stiff fingers first."

"Ethan. Sit down – listen. I told you I have an idea."

It was all he could do to bite back the torrent of curses that wanted to spill from his lips. Damn Lacey and Carl to hell. He'd spend the rest of his days in a federal penitentiary rather than allow them to take over his ranch. He pulled the chair upright and carefully sat back down.

"I know you're upset. I was, too, but I talked to Matt about my idea and he thinks it's a good one. Are you calm enough to hear me out?"

He wanted to kick himself for losing his temper when all Autumn was trying to do was help. What kind of husband would he be if the first sign of trouble sent him throwing chairs and swearing up a blue streak? He had to do better than that.

"I'll behave," he said and let the corner of his lips quirk up. Her expression softened and she met his gaze with shining eyes.

"A guest ranch." She waited for his reaction.

"Hmm?"

"A guest ranch! We turn the Big House into guest accommodations and make money off of tourists!"

He sat back, a frown thinning his lips.

"Hear me out," Autumn said. "It doesn't have to interfere with the normal running of the ranch at all. You barely have to be involved if you don't want to be – we can hire people to do most of the work with the guests. You and Jamie and the rest of the hands just need to be around looking…I don't know – cowboy-ish, you know?"

"You want me and Jamie to be tourist attractions?"

"For heaven's sake, there are guest ranches all over Montana. Surely you know someone who has one." She looked exasperated.

Ethan forced himself to think over her words. Yes, he did know people who owned guest ranches. He'd just never considered the idea for himself before. He'd always expected to have his father's help running cattle, and that his income would always come from that line of work. "I wouldn't have to lead trail rides?" he said warily.

"Not if you're dead set against it. Of course, the more work we keep in the family, the more money we make."

"Won't there be a passel of start up costs?"

"Not as much as you might think." She tossed him a pile of paper. "I've outlined all the numbers in there. I made a budget for the next three years with some income projections and so on. The Big House is already gorgeous – and with all its bedrooms and bathrooms it's basically set up for accommodating guests already. The kitchen is professional grade and the dining room seats plenty of people. With us living in the bunkhouse there's plenty of space for paying customers. That is, if you're comfortable with people being in the Big House…" She trailed off, seeming nervous again. After a second, Ethan realized why.

"I'm all right with that," he assured her. "After my parents died I didn't want to live there alone, but I don't mind if other people use it."

"You might have to eat some dinners there," she warned. "Entertain the guests with cowboy stories."

"I can probably do that once in a while."

141

"We will need some money," Autumn warned him, "and we'll need to buy Claire out. Matt has an idea for that. He said he has a buyer – not Lacey and Carl – who is interested in purchasing one hundred acres in the southeast corner. If we sell, we'll have enough money to secure a second mortgage so we can pay off Claire. Things will be tight for a long time, but eventually we'll get back in the black."

"Who's the buyer?"

"I don't know. He said it might take a week or two for the buyer to get his money together, but it sounds like he's definitely interested. We'll have to figure out a way to hold off Claire until then."

He would call Matt in the morning and find out who the mystery buyer was. "Claire can't sell until I agree to; if she wants to take me to court over it the process will drag on for months. I'll tell her to give me a couple of weeks to pull things together." Ethan stared at Autumn, his pizza all but forgotten. "Why are you doing all of this?" he asked. He must be dreaming. For so long his life had been bad news followed by disasters, and now this woman – this angel – had appeared out of nowhere and set everything to rights in such a short time. How was he supposed to believe it could last?

"Because this is where I want to raise our family, Ethan."

"We're really doing this?" He leaned forward and took Autumn's hand. It was soft and small, but he now knew she would make a capable partner for his life's journey.

"Yes."

"We're getting married in twenty-one days?"

"Yes." She nodded. "We'd better start planning. I need a dress and flowers…"

"What you need," Ethan said. "Is to get over here and let me take you to bed."

Chapter Eleven

According to the phone book, Ellie's Bridals was the only store in Chance Creek that carried wedding gowns. Autumn parked Ethan's truck outside the boutique with trepidation and remained in the driver's seat a moment to look the little store over. She'd always thought she'd spend days trolling through New York City with her friends trying on dresses when it came time for her to be married. She'd pictured sales ladies in haute couture serving her champagne from silver trays while she posed in front of floor length mirrors in the latest style.

As a young girl, she favored dresses with trains a mile long. At twenty she would have picked something severe and sophisticated. What did one wear to a country wedding?

She gripped the steering wheel with hands that were suddenly sweaty. What was she doing? She hadn't even told her mother or sister or even her best friend what was happening and she was supposed to get married in less than three weeks. Becka had texted her once or twice, then reverted to email when she realized Autumn wasn't carrying her cell phone with her everywhere like she normally did. She'd told Becka some of the details about the ranch and gardening and cooking, and how hot Ethan was, but she'd neglected to say anything about sleeping with the man. For one thing, it didn't sound very professional. For another, she didn't want to face Becka's tough questions.

Tonight she and Ethan would have to sit down and make some plans. Guest lists, catering…her head began to swim and she rested her forehead on the steering wheel. She needed to call her editor, too – tell her she wasn't coming back. Panic gripped her. Was she ready to burn her bridges like that?

"Autumn? Is everything okay?"

She reared back with a gasp. "Rose! You scared me to death!"

Rose stood on tiptoe just outside the open window of the Ford F-250. "Sorry! You looked like you were going to be sick. Is everything okay?"

"I…yes. I think it is. I'm…" she glanced at the boutique. "Picking out my wedding dress."

"Oh, my gosh! That's so exciting!" Rose peeked into the cab of the truck. "All alone? Isn't anyone going to help you?"

"I don't know anyone in town." Rose's tone said it all – it was pathetic to shop alone for your wedding dress. Maybe she should have called Becka to see if she could fly in for a day or two. But then she'd have to explain everything.

"I've got some time. Can I come with you? I love looking at wedding gowns, and I've got a good eye!"

Rose bounced on the soles of her feet and Autumn found herself smiling at the young woman. Why not? After all, she'd done a great job helping them pick out the diamond ring that sparkled on her finger.

"Please do! I was dreading going in there by myself." She gathered her purse and let herself out of the truck, locking it behind her. When she turned toward the shop she caught Rose's smirk. "What?"

"City girl – no one locks their cars here." Rose linked her arm through Autumn's and pulled her toward the store. "Come on, this is going to be a blast!"

Half an hour later, Autumn was thrilled she was in Chance Creek rather than New York. Ellie's Bridals was run by Ellie Donaldson, a boisterous sixty-something-year-old with a biting sense of humor that had Rose and Autumn nearly in tears as she told stories of weddings past – both triumphs and disasters. The little boutique was crammed full of gowns. The minute Autumn walked through the door Ellie took her measure and pronounced she had just the thing.

Just the thing turned out to be armloads of dresses Ellie hung on a wire rack outside a hexagonal dressing room hidden toward the back of the store. She and Rose took turns helping Autumn into and out of the gowns and leading her to the pedestal in the center of a room with mirrors positioned carefully to reflect her from every angle.

They vetoed the majority of dresses before she even set foot out of the dressing room, but several possibilities had accumulated on a second metal rack.

"This is the one I really wanted you to try," Ellie said, holding out what looked like a very simple gown. "I knew it was perfect the moment you walked in the door, but brides have to try on lots of dresses or they won't be satisfied. Here – give this one a whirl."

Rose helped her out of a lace covered prairie-style gown they'd all agreed looked absolutely hideous and slid the smooth satin dress over her head. The bodice was fitted, with a sophisticated draped front neckline and plunging back. The skirt clung to her curves, folds of fabric falling to the floor in an abbreviated train. She felt like a 1940s movie star.

"Wow," Rose breathed. "You're a knockout. Ethan won't know what hit him when he sees you in this."

Ellie nodded happily. "I told you – just the thing." She helped Autumn up onto the pedestal and stood back while she drank in the picture of this new, incredibly sensual version of herself. Somehow the dress echoed the way Ethan made her feel – curvy, sexy and beautiful.

When the bell over the door jangled and someone walked in, they all needed a moment before they could return to the present.

"Take your time looking, dearie. I'll see who's out front," Ellie said, leaving the inner sanctum of the changing area for the front of the store.

"Hi Ellie! I hope you aren't busy, because I plan to monopolize you for the rest of the afternoon. I'll be ordering my real wedding dress from Paris, of course, but I want to try on every gown you have to get ideas of what I don't want."

Autumn's heart plummeted into the pit of her stomach at the familiar strident tones.

Lacey.

It figured.

Rose met her gaze and made a face. They both heard Ellie say, "Sorry, my dear – I'm already helping a customer and we'll probably be some time yet. Maybe you'd like to come back after lunch when I can give you my full attention?"

"That won't work for me at all. This afternoon I'm picking out floral arrangements – I have a schedule to keep! Who's here with you? Maybe they can come back."

Autumn heard footsteps approaching and jumped down from the pedestal, rushing for the changing room, her feet tangling in the train of her gown. Rose grabbed her arm and kept her upright as Lacey burst through racks of wedding gowns and into view. She narrowed her eyes, face flooding with angry color at the sight of them.

"You! What are you doing here?"

"What do you think she's doing?" Rose said, stepping in front of Autumn. "She's choosing a wedding dress – duh!"

"For what? You aren't getting married! Didn't you hear a thing I said at the diner? Ethan's broke and Carl's buying his ranch for me, so you'll have nothing if you marry that loser – nothing!"

"Why do you care so much if you think Ethan's a loser?" Autumn said, peering around Rose. "Why don't you just leave us alone?"

"Because…" Lacey sputtered. "Because you're ruining everything! Everyone is supposed to be focused on my wedding – it's going to be the event of the year! And instead all they're talking about is you. Why don't you go home to New York – you don't belong here, and you definitely don't belong with Ethan!"

"No," Ellie said, puffing her grandmotherly bosom out like the prow a battleship. "You're the one who doesn't belong here, Lacey Turner. I don't even recognize you anymore. When you were a little girl you were the sweetest thing. Now look what you've turned into. Only a truly wicked woman dumps the man she loves in the moment of his biggest defeat and then adds insult to injury by trying to turn others against him. Marriage is the joining of a man and a woman forever – for richer or poorer. That's what wedding vows say. I doubt you've ever paid attention to the wording, though, since you're much too busy calculating how much money it will net you. You ought to be ashamed of yourself, and I'm ashamed to have you in my store. I sell wedding gowns to brides here – I don't cater to…to…fortune hunters."

149

Autumn's mouth dropped open at the older woman's tirade. A moment later Lacey turned on her heel and marched out the front door.

"Good riddance," Rose said.

Ellie bustled over to a dress rack. "I think we all know you've picked your gown, but you try on a few more, just to be sure." She held out a gown with a beaded bodice.

Autumn took it and dutifully turned so Rose could unbutton her current one, but her joy in the morning had gone out the door with Lacey.

The next week and a half flew by in a blur until Saturday rolled around again, and only a week remained until her wedding. In between fittings for her dress and all the other arrangements, she hardly had time to consider the drastic step she was taking. She also had very little time to worry about the fact that she still hadn't told her mother, sister, or even Becka about the big event. But now with only seven days left until the ceremony, she knew she couldn't put it off any longer. Ethan brought it up once, when they were coming up with numbers for Rose, who had volunteered to coordinate a potluck buffet dinner to hold down costs. About sixty people would attend the wedding, almost all of them Ethan's friends and neighbors from Chance Creek. Aside from Becka and her family, Autumn couldn't think of anyone to invite. She had plenty of acquaintances, but few real friends she'd ask to buy a plane ticket just to see her walk down the aisle.

"Your Mom and sister will be there, right?" he said. "I have to meet your family."

"Of course they will – they wouldn't miss it for the world," she said.

But she hadn't picked up the phone or sent an invitation. Now she had no choice.

She called Becka first.

"Ohmygod, Autumn! Where've you been – I was about to send the police after you!" Becka squealed.

"I know – I'm sorry. Things got really crazy here, really fast. You won't believe what's happened."

"What, you're going to marry the cowboy?" Becka laughed. Autumn, stunned, remained silent. A pause stretched out. "No way. Autumn – you're not serious. You're marrying him? You've known him, what – three weeks?"

"I know it's crazy, but you have to meet him, Becks – he's amazing. He's so handsome and kind and wonderful."

"He'd better be wonderful," Becka said after a long moment. "If he's stealing you away from me he'd better be awesome. Crap, you're not coming back to New York, are you? Autumn – I'll never see you again."

"Sorry," Autumn said in a small voice. "I'm staying here. I love it. The ranch is so beautiful – better than anything we pictured and we're going to turn it into a guest ranch. There's an amazing lodge basically all ready for people to come and stay. That's where we'll put you when you come out for the wedding."

"When is it?"

"Next Saturday." Autumn held her breath. Becka's voice screeched over the line, "Next Saturday? Are you insane? That's...next Saturday! You can't marry him that fast."

"The minister's already booked and I have my dress."

"I thought I'd be there when you picked out your dress," Becka said. Autumn heard the hurt in her friend's voice and sunk a little lower on the guest room bed where she'd retreated to make the call.

"I know – I'm sorry. Like I said, this all happened really fast. So can you come out on Wednesday and we'll shop for your bridesmaid gown together? You can pick any one you want – on me! We'll find you something really gorgeous and you can dance with all the cowboys at the reception. Pretty please? Don't be mad – I still have to call Mom and Lily."

"You haven't told your mother you're getting married next week?" Becka shrieked again.

"Can you blame me? Can you imagine her reaction?"

"Yeah – she's going to think you got knocked up and needed a shotgun wedding." Becka paused. "Oh, no. Autumn, don't tell me you got knocked up."

"I didn't get knocked up! I mean, I don't think..." She dropped a hand to her belly. "Okay, you can't tell anyone about this."

152

Becka groaned. "Lay it on me."

"We didn't use protection the first time we had sex. And I'm kind of late – just a couple of days, nothing drastic."

"What the hell are you waiting for – why haven't you taken a pregnancy test?"

"I'm going to – tonight. It's been so busy and I haven't felt nauseous in the mornings, so I'm good, right?"

"I don't know, honey – go pee on that stick and we'll find out together."

"I wish I could, but I want to save it until Ethan gets home."

"You're not just marrying him because you might be pregnant, though, are you?" Becka asked.

"No. Definitely not. I'm head over heels for this guy, Becka. I never thought I'd be this happy."

"Then I guess I'm happy for you," she said, although she didn't sound completely convinced. "Give me the details and I'll buy my ticket right now."

Five minutes later, she clicked off the phone and stared at it, willing herself the courage to dial her mother's cell number. The conversation wasn't going to be pretty – she'd told her mother she was here researching a story, but left the details deliberately vague, so her news was going to come entirely out of left field. She took a deep breath and punched in the number.

"Hi, Mom," she said when Teresa picked up.

"Autumn! Hi, honey – where are you?"

"I'm still in Montana, working on that...thing," she began and then wanted to knock her head against the wall. "But something's happened."

"What is it? I have to hurry, I'm on my way into the office."

Autumn could picture her mother rushing around her ultra-modern townhouse, finding her shoes and her purse and her briefcase.

"I'm getting married," she blurted. "Next Saturday. He's a cowboy and I love him and we're going to run a guest ranch and I totally love him. Can you make the wedding? We can put you up." She bit her lip and waited for Teresa's reaction.

Her mother appeared to have lost her voice. After a couple of strangled noises, she finally cleared her throat. "Did you just say you're getting married?"

"Yes."

"To whom?"

"His name is Ethan Cruz. He owns a ranch here in Montana." Autumn bit her lip and hunched lower on the bed, every muscle in her body clenched in anticipation of her mother's next words.

"You're getting married to a man who owns a ranch in Montana."

"Yes."

"How long ago did you meet this Ethan Cruz?" Teresa' voice was icy cold. Damn, that wasn't good.

"Three weeks ago."

"And he owns a ranch."

"A cattle ranch, yes."

"This is a profitable ranch?"

"Umm…" *Shit*! "It's got a few problems, but we've figured out a way to…"

"And the wedding is next week."

"Yes, but…"

"A week from today you're marrying a man you barely know who owns an unprofitable ranch in Montana. Do I have that right?"

"Yes," Autumn whispered. This was going worse than she expected.

"That is the stupidest thing I've ever heard. You get your ass on the next plane back home – tonight – or I'm sending Lily there after you. You're going to tell that insolvent cowboy to get back on the horse he rode in on, and we're going to sort out your future once and for all. There's still time for you to get your master's degree. You can get your MBA, if you're so keen on working in the hospitality business. I don't know why we didn't think of it sooner."

"Mom…"

"Now, Autumn. Do I make myself clear? You get on that plane right NOW."

A tear spilled down her cheek. "No, Mom. I'm not coming home. I love Ethan, and his financial situation is just fine – we've already figured out exactly what we're going to do. I'm getting married next Saturday at 4 o'clock in the afternoon right here at Ethan's ranch, and I'd love for you and Lily to be here – but only if you come to support me. I don't need any more lectures about the right way or wrong way to live my life. It's my life, Mom. I'm choosing what I want to do. I'll email you all the information. I hope you'll come and walk me down the aisle, since Daddy won't be here to do it."

She hung up before her mother could answer and walked on unsteady legs out to the back porch. She lived here in Chance Creek now and this ranch and the nearby town would be her home from here on out. Maybe she wouldn't have any family attending her wedding, after all, but the rest of the guests would soon be her friends if she had any say in it. This was where she was making her stand. Here with Ethan on the Cruz family ranch.

Chapter Twelve

"Good to see you, Matt, but I still don't understand why you couldn't answer my questions over the phone," Ethan said as he took the chair Matt offered him in front of the large, walnut desk.

"I'll explain everything." Matt took his own seat but left the door to his office open, presumably because his secretary wasn't in and he wanted to see his mystery buyer when he arrived.

"So who is this guy who wants my 100 acres?" Ethan said, settling back in the chair.

"Before we get into that, let's talk about Autumn's idea. I'm assuming she's filled you in on everything. Did you get a chance to read over her numbers?"

"Yep." Ethan nodded. "Looks like a good idea, as long as I can stay concentrating on the cattle and the day to day operations of the ranch. I'm not what you'd call a social butterfly, and I don't think I'd be all that good at riding herd on a bunch of tourists. Autumn says as long as I make an appearance now and then and tell a few stories to the guests in the evenings, it'll be all right. She wants to handle the cooking and supplies, and we'll hire people to help out both in the lodge and to entertain guests with trail rides and chores." He used finger quotes to express his opinion of this last part. A bunch of greenhorns wouldn't be a lot of help with the cattle, but he was sure he could come up with something to keep them busy and out of trouble.

"I think it's a terrific idea. There are lots of successful guest ranches in Montana, but none in Chance Creek that I know of. Your Big House has a terrific view and as far as I remember it's the lap of luxury inside."

"Thanks to Momma," Ethan said wryly.

"So what you need is a little ready cash for starting up and a means to buy out Claire – am I right?"

"That about sums it up. Think we can swing it?"

"I do. I took the liberty of calling Claire and setting up a meeting later. Meanwhile, I think our buyer for your acres has arrived. I've done up the paperwork for the sale and for buying out Claire. If all goes well, we'll plow through it all this morning."

"You work fast," Ethan said, surprised.

"I felt it behooved us for me to do so. Claire has another buyer lined up for the ranch – the whole ranch."

Ethan looked away. "Lacey," he said, his jaw tight. "I heard."

"Claire's more than a little miffed that you keep putting her off and she let me know about it. I figured it would be best for everyone concerned to avoid that outcome," Matt said. He glanced out the door ."Good, he's here – let's get started."

You could have knocked Ethan over with a feather when Jamie walked in, the same grin plastered on his face that stole the hearts of every woman within a hundred miles. "Hey, Ethan."

"Jamie. What're you doing here?"

"Looking to buy me some land. Actually, I'm looking for more than that. Matt will explain." He took the other chair in the office and tipped it back, resting one booted foot atop his other leg, supremely confident, as usual. Nothing ever seemed to faze Jamie.

Ethan wished he felt anywhere near as confident. He turned to Matt. "I'm listening."

"Jamie, here, has saved up a fair whack of cash," Matt began. "Seems he should have been an investment banker rather than a cowboy."

"My Daddy tried his damndest to make me one," Jamie interjected. "Didn't take."

Ethan suppressed a smile. He hadn't thought about that in ages. Poor Jamie had spent four years sweating it out at Montana State while the rest of them got right to living after high school. He'd hated every minute of it and spent every available weekend and summer on the Cruz Ranch working with Ethan and his dad until he felt more like a brother than a friend. The minute he graduated with his BA in Business Administration, he'd booked it back to the ranch and hadn't left since. Jamie was the quintessential cowboy, as far as Ethan was concerned. He lived and breathed horses and was one of the best ranch hands he'd ever worked with. The idea of him working a desk job was laughable.

"Some of it took," Matt said. "You've done a terrific job with your investments."

Jamie shrugged. "Don't have much call to spend my money."

Ethan laughed out loud. "That's for sure. You ever been with Jamie at the bar?" he asked Matt. "Ever seen him buy a round? Jamie puts the cheap in cheapskate. Everybody knows that!"

"It worked, didn't it?" Jamie said, some of the smugness gone from his face. "I've got enough cash to secure a loan to buy 100 acres of your land."

"What're you going to do with it?" Ethan asked.

"Breed horses."

"You won't work for me no more?"

Jamie studied the painting behind Matt's desk. "I'd like to work *with* you. I'd like to buy in to a share of the ranch and keep the property as a single parcel. Matt told me about Autumn's idea and I think it's a terrific one. I wouldn't mind working with the guests – teaching them to ride, taking them out on day trips. Maybe taking groups out for week-long camping trips out on the range. I like that kind of thing."

"You wouldn't mind dealing with all those people?"

A smile curved Jamie's lips. "I like people."

"You like women. What about their husbands and children?"

"I reckon I can tolerate a few of them, too. I like teaching people stuff. I like the idea of getting kids away from their computers and out into the real world. Can you imagine what it'd be like to put a kid on a horse for the first time and lead them out into the country? I think that's gotta be better than us losing the ranch and having to work for Carl."

Ethan's knuckles tightened reflexively on the armrests of his chair. "You got that right." He studied Jamie. "I didn't realize you loved the ranch that much."

Jamie bristled. "I helped build those fences alongside you and your Daddy. I was out there every second I could – helping birth the foals, training all those horses. I may not be blood, but you can't deny my sweat's been poured over every inch of that land!"

"Whoa! I wasn't attacking you." Ethan stood up and held out his hand to Jamie. "I was welcoming you." The outer door to the office opened and someone came in, but Jamie stood up, too, and blocked his view.

He hesitated. "You saying you'll sell to me?"

"I'm saying I can't think of anyone else I'd want as a business partner. I'd be proud to co-own the ranch with you."

He was about to shake Jamie's hand when Claire stormed into the office. "What the hell is going on here? You can't sell a partnership to the ranch! I'm half owner, and I'm selling the whole thing to Lacey and Carl!"

"Claire," Matt got between them and held out a hand. "Thanks for coming. Sit down." He cleared his throat and Jamie quickly moved away from his chair to make it available to her.

"I'm not going to sit down until I know what the hell's going on here." She crossed her arms over her chest, her sleek bob swinging.

"Calm down, Claire – it's good news. I'm buying you out. You'll have enough money to open up a whole chain of interior design businesses," Ethan said.

Her gaze swept from Ethan to Matt to Jamie. "Really? I'll get half the price of the ranch?" She sat down and faced Matt. "Tell me."

"Six hundred-thousand dollars," Matt said, drawing a sheaf of papers out of a file folder. "Jamie's buying a quarter share in the ranch, and together they'll qualify for a second mortgage that will buy you out. When everything's settled and signed, you'll have your money and Ethan and Jamie will own the ranch."

"And Autumn," Ethan said.

"And Autumn, just as soon as the two of you are married," Matt agreed.

"Oh, my God," Claire said. "I didn't think…I had no idea…" She turned to Ethan. "But you'll be up to your eyeballs in debt!"

"I'm already up to my eyeballs in debt," Ethan said. "But Autumn came up with a great idea. We're going to open the Big House as a guest ranch. She loves to cook and she's amazing at it. She wants to feed the guests, and Jamie here wants to handle the outside chores – teaching guests to ride, and all that. I'll keep running the ranch like I've always done and we'll hire some kids from town to do the rest."

Claire blinked. "That's…a really good idea."

"Don't sound so surprised," Ethan said, sitting back in his chair. "My bride's pretty smart."

Claire looked skeptical. "If she's so smart why would she pick you for a husband?"

"Ouch!" Ethan scowled and Claire grinned. For a second his sister looked like her old self, before she'd grown up and gone boy crazy, before all the fights with their mother. God, he missed those days.

"You sure you don't want to go in on the business with us?" Jamie asked Claire. "You could help out with the horses, too. Teach kids to ride?"

Now it was Ethan's turn to blink. It was like Jamie had read his mind and also remembered Claire as she used to be – crazy for riding and one of the best in the entire county at it. But as far as he knew Claire hadn't been on a horse since she hightailed it to Billings years ago. She hated the ranch and everything about it; he just wished he knew why. Sure, she'd fought like cats and dogs with their mother during her teenage years, but that was water way under the bridge. Maybe it wasn't for Claire, though. She hadn't made up with her mother before their parents' deaths.

"No thanks. I'm going to take the money and run," Claire said. "If I were you, Ethan, I'd steer clear of Lacey for a long, long time. She's going to be furious. She was really looking forward to rubbing your nose into the fact that she owned our ranch."

"I can't believe you would have sold it to her," Ethan said.

"I can't believe you don't know how much I hate that place," Claire said. "But then you never noticed much except for that land and those cattle, did you?"

Ethan frowned as she bent over the paperwork, and exchanged a confused glance behind her back with Jamie. Jamie seemed just as much in the dark as he was. Something had happened to Claire in those turbulent teenage years to turn her into a different person. Seeing his own troubled feelings echoed in Jamie's worried look he felt a pang. This wasn't the first time he'd wondered if his friend harbored feelings for his sister, and if Claire hadn't turned into such a stick-in-the-mud city girl – 29 going on 45 – he'd welcome the match.

He shrugged at Jamie and turned back to Matt. During the next hour they negotiated the terms of Jamie's purchase and Claire's sale and it was with a huge sense of relief that he exited the building, Jamie and Claire in tow.

"How about we celebrate tonight at the Dancing Boot?" Jamie asked. "I know I'm sure in the mood for a few drinks and maybe a little dancing!"

"I'm in – I'm sure Autumn will be, too," Ethan said.

"What about you, Claire?" Jamie asked. "Come on – you haven't been out with us in ages!"

"When have I ever been out with you, Jamie?" she retorted. "I'm not going to drink and then drive all the way back to Billings. Besides I've got houses to decorate."

Jamie rolled his eyes. "Go do your work, baby girl, then come on back and have dinner with me. We'll meet everyone else at the bar and take it from there. If you're too chicken to sleep on my couch I'm sure you can sleep on Ethan's."

"I'm way too old to sleep on anyone's couch," Claire said. "I'll see you guys around." She headed for her car, but Jamie took her arm and pulled her to a halt.

"Claire. Have dinner with me – I'm celebrating tonight and so is Ethan. This is a big deal to us."

Ethan waited for her answer, curious to see how this would play out. There was no way she would agree, but then again, it was Jamie talking and he did have a way with the women.

She tapped her toe on the sidewalk, then sighed. "All right, I'll meet you for dinner. I'm not staying out late, though. And I'm not sleeping on anyone's couch!"

"I'll walk you to your car," Jamie said and winked at Ethan over Claire's shoulder. Ethan supposed he should feel worried about his sister's honor, but Claire could definitely take care of herself – even with Jamie.

He headed for his own truck, eager to tell Autumn his good news.

"Hey – anybody home?"

Autumn jumped when a man's voice boomed through the bunkhouse. She was in the spare bedroom getting dressed for their night out on the town, and from the sound of things Ethan was still in the shower. He'd come home from the accountant's office, swept her into his arms and kissed her before explaining about Jamie becoming a partner in the ranch and being able to buy Claire out.

She quickly zipped her jeans, pulled the shirt she'd laid out over her head, smoothed it down and poked her head out of the bedroom door.

"Who is it?"

"It's Rob – is Ethan here?"

She walked into the kitchen. "He's in the shower. Can I help you?" She kept the length of the kitchen between them, still mindful of the gossip Rose had told her when she picked out her ring, about how he'd tried to film himself having sex with Rose's friend's cousin.

"Just came to see if you all wanted to join me for dinner before hitting the bar. I'm starved – man's gotta fortify himself for the night to come and all that."

"Uh …" Autumn tried to hide her disappointment. She was all set to take the pregnancy test just as soon as Ethan got out of the shower. She had pictured them waiting for the results together, hand in hand, and then celebrating afterward with a romantic dinner for two, but it turned out Ethan already invited Claire and Jamie along. Now Rob was joining them, too?

"Rob! Good to see you! You coming to dinner with us?" Ethan appeared, towel wrapped around his waist.

"I heard there was celebrating to be done – and I'm always up for a celebration! I heard you're buying Claire out of her share of the ranch."

"You heard right," Ethan said.

"And Jamie's going to be your new partner?"

"Yep."

"Well, that beats everything. Who knew that little cheapskate was piling up his money in order to pull this off. You oughta be grateful you needed to sell now – a couple more years and he'd have bought the whole damn thing out from under you."

"I'm hoping he sets his smarts to the business and makes me rich," Ethan said.

"He just might." Rob cocked his head. "And I hear the two of you are making a serious go at this getting married thing. Buying wedding gowns, making guest lists…"

"It's only a week away," Autumn said, taking Ethan's arm. He gave her a squeeze and she tried smile, but she was still disappointed her dinner with Ethan was turning into such a crowd affair.

Rob scratched his head. "Who would've thought running a want ad on Youtube would end up with you finding the woman of your dreams?"

Ethan stiffened beside her and when he answered there was an edge to his voice. "Yeah, who would've thought? Let's get going, I thought you were starving."

"I am, buddy – I am."

Autumn frowned. She had a feeling there was more to that interchange than she was comprehending.

She turned to Ethan with an eyebrow raised. He evaded her gaze and headed back toward the bedroom.

"I just need a minute. You almost ready, Autumn?"

"Uh…I guess."

"Let's start at DelMonaco's. I need a steak," Rob proclaimed.

"Sounds good."

"I need a minute, too." Autumn followed Ethan back to the bedroom and shut the door behind her. The sight of him shucking off his towel and reaching for a fresh pair of jeans distracted her, but only for a moment. "Hey, I thought…I kind of hoped it'd be just the two of us at dinner tonight. Now we're at five."

Ethan turned toward her, and her stomach did another flip-flop at his muscular chest and flat belly, not to mention…

"Honey, I don't think it'll even be just the five of us for very long. When word gets out that I'm keeping the ranch and that Jamie's my new business partner – our new business partner – we'll have half the town celebrating with us." He moved closer, jeans still dangling from one hand. "But we'll have lots of time alone together later tonight. I promise."

Autumn's disappointment over not being able to take the pregnancy test soon melted away beneath his kisses. A few more hours wouldn't make much of a difference. They'd come home, she'd take the test and then they'd go straight to bed. It could be worse. In an instant, she was in his arms, pressed up close against him, and they probably wouldn't have made it out the door to dinner anytime soon if Rob hadn't hollered from the kitchen, "Hurry up in there or I'm coming in after you! I'm starving!"

They broke apart, laughing, and Ethan quickly pulled on boxers and jeans. In another minute they'd rejoined Rob and were on their way.

Chapter Thirteen

DelMonaco's was packed as usual when Ethan pulled the Ford up beside Rob's Chevy in the parking lot. They didn't even make it to the door before Jamie yelled for them to wait up. Autumn turned to see him leading Claire by the hand across the parking lot from the other direction.

"Jamie, Claire!" Rob called. "Perfect timing!"

Claire hung back a little as Jamie led her up the steps, as if she was embarrassed, Autumn thought, but the noisy greetings of the men covered up any awkwardness and soon the whole group was seated at a table.

No sooner had their waitress brought the first round of drinks when Cab appeared. "Is this a private party, or can anyone join in?" He didn't wait for an answer – just grabbed a chair from a nearby table and sat down.

Before long a whole crowd had joined them and the waitresses kept busy pushing tables together and bringing more chairs. Ethan caught on right away that Autumn didn't want to drink and helped mask her abstention by switching glasses with her when he'd drained one. Rob seemed to be drinking the most of all and managed to make about half of the noise himself. Autumn wondered what was eating him. For all his laughter and toasts and cheers to Ethan and Jamie's good fortune, she sensed he wasn't happy at all. In fact, she couldn't entirely understand the friendship between Ethan and Rob. Everyone said they were best friends, but how could honorable Ethan be so close to a man who would try to lure unsuspecting women into making porno movies? And if Rob liked Ethan so much, why would he be so angry tonight when Ethan was celebrating. She turned back to her meal, resolved to keep an eye on the situation.

Most of the men ordered steak, the women chicken. Autumn ordered eggplant parmesan and then poked at it, decidedly not hungry. She was just as pleased as everyone else about the progress they'd made on keeping the ranch, but she was way too distracted by the thought of the pregnancy test kit stashed in her luggage back at the bunkhouse to truly get into the celebratory mood.

Claire looked different tonight, she thought as she pushed a bite around the perimeter of her plate. She looked…younger. Happier. Must be the thought of all that money pouring into her bank account. What would she do with six hundred thousand dollars, if it was hers? Her gaze rested on Ethan. Invest it into the ranch, most likely. Her attention returned to Claire. She realized it was the woman's outfit that made her seem different tonight. Gone were the stiff-looking business skirt and blouse, the sensible shoes, and in their place she wore form fitting jeans and a peasant blouse. Jamie couldn't take his eyes off of her, she noticed with a grin. Was romance blooming there?

As she finally lifted the bite of eggplant to her mouth, she caught sight of Rob's face. He, too, was watching Jamie and Claire, but his expression was hard. The hand holding his fork clenched tightly. But a moment later, he turned back to his meal and popped a piece of steak into his mouth. By the time he'd chewed and swallowed, he was back to faking good spirits, joking around with Cab, who sat across from him. Autumn shook her head. She barely knew these people. How could she translate the undercurrents swirling around her?

When the waitress returned to clear their plates, talk at the table turned to what to do with the rest of the evening.

"I thought we were heading to the Dancing Boot," Jamie said. "I promised Claire we'd close the place down."

"Sounds good to me," Ethan said. "What about you, Autumn?"

"Sure." She bit her lip, thinking of the pregnancy test again. Still, this night was a big deal to Ethan. She'd find out whether or not she was pregnant soon enough.

"Rob, Cab? You guys coming with us?" Ethan asked.

"Sure thing," Cab said. "I've got nowhere else to be."

Rob made a face. "Ain't no point me going with you. Not like anyone's going to dance with me tonight."

Claire laughed out loud and more than one person at the table looked surprised. "Are you kidding, Rob? Since when have you lacked for partners – you always have some girl or other on your arm. Always have!"

"Not anymore. Not since this joker," he stabbed a finger at Ethan, "pulled his last trick."

"Uh oh," Claire said. "More practical jokes? I thought you guys would have given that up by now."

"What did Ethan do?" Autumn asked. Rose had said something about practical jokes back when they were buying her engagement ring, but she couldn't imagine steady, solid Ethan planning out a complicated joke.

"Let me tell her! You gotta let me tell her," Jamie said, his face splitting into a wide grin. Rob waved him off at first, then sat back as if giving up. "First, you gotta understand these guys have been playing tricks on each other since grade school – this ain't nothing new. Rob deserved everything he got."

"I didn't deserve..." Rob began but everyone shouted him down.

"As I was saying," Jamie said. "He deserved it. Ethan was looking for payback for a trick Rob played on him a couple of months ago."

Ethan leaned forward. "Not just a trick. He moved all the cattle out of the northwest pasture onto his own land and left the fence all torn apart to make it look like someone stole them. Scared me half to death. That pasture doesn't border Rob's property," he explained to Autumn, "so it didn't occur to me at first it was him. What with all my debts, losing any of the herd would have put me under. I called the police, the sheriff's office," he nodded toward Cab, "I was about to call the CIA before I realized it was probably Rob playing a joke on me. Nearly gave me a heart attack."

Appreciative laughter came from around the table as Jamie took up the thread of the story again. "So Ethan, here, makes a plan and bides his time. It's kind of an ingenious plan, too. Rob's a bit of a ladies' man."

"That's an understatement," Claire said.

"He tends to make friends on the dance floor," Jamie said. "Good friends. Hardly ever goes home alone on a Saturday night. Ethan was counting on that, so when a Saturday night came up and he saw Rob getting it on with a fine, young thing out on the dance floor, he nipped out early, rode over to Rob's cabin, and snuck inside."

"What did he do?" Autumn said when Jamie hesitated.

"Well," Jamie said, his grin getting even wider. "He set up a big, ol' video camera on a tripod at the end of Rob's bed, hung up this backdrop he'd painted on a bed sheet – what did you paint again?"

174

"A barn with a bunch of horses running around," Ethan said. "The view from my back porch!"

More laughter all around.

"He hung up the backdrop by the bed, and set up these big old lamps all around with their shades topsy turvy like lights on a movie set," Jamie broke off laughing and Autumn felt her own lips curl up with the beginnings of a smile – she knew exactly where this was going. "So when Rob brought that lovely lady of his home and eased her into the bedroom, she about nearly had a fit! You could have heard her screaming in Billings!"

"She thought I wanted to make a porno flick!" Rob said, the only one at the table not laughing. "She screamed bloody murder – I was afraid for my life!"

That only made the crowd laugh harder, Autumn right along with them. She knew from the seriousness with which Rose had told the story to her that her friend's cousin had bought the ruse hook, line and sinker.

"She hightailed it out of there so fast I couldn't explain anything, and she's told everyone about it – every woman in a hundred mile radius thinks I'm a freak now. I haven't had a date – or even a dance – in a month! It's not funny!"

Even Autumn couldn't keep the tears from rolling down her face, and normally she didn't hold with practical jokes. The thought of this suave Lothario getting his comeuppance was too much to bear, though.

"Fine. Go ahead and laugh, see if I care."

But as Autumn regained control she could see Rob did care. He sat back and played with his drink, but didn't lift it to his mouth. He seemed lost in thought and whatever he was thinking wasn't pleasant.

"Oh, come on, Rob – you sure got me back good," Ethan said, then froze. Cab and Jamie froze, too. Rob looked from one to the other and straightened up.

"Yeah, that's right – I did get you back good, didn't I?"

Confused by the sudden tension around the table, Autumn said, "What? What did you do?"

There was a long moment of silence, then Rob smiled slowly. "That particular joke hasn't had its run just yet, so I think I'll let sleeping dogs lie. Right, Ethan? You think that's a good call?"

"I think that's a great call, Rob," Ethan said in a tight voice. "And I think we should finish up here and get over to the Dancing Boot. Ladies, have pity on Rob here – the man needs a dance partner. Bad."

The tension broken, people began to make their way toward the exit.

"What was that all about?" Autumn asked Ethan as she linked her arm through his and walked out to the Ford.

"Ignore Rob. He tried to get back at me and then found out the joke was on him again."

Autumn managed to forget Rob's strange behavior and the pregnancy test waiting at home for several hours after they moved the party over to the Dancing Boot. Ethan taught her the two-step and swung her around the room during song after song until she was dizzy and breathless and had to sit down. When the line dancing started she begged off, but had a great time watching the fancy footwork of the others. Jamie was particularly light on his feet and Claire wasn't half bad, either. They made an interesting couple, she thought, now that Claire had lightened up a little.

Cab sat out the line dancing, too, but he'd taken his turn as her partner for a couple of other dances and she enjoyed his company, both on the dance floor and off. He told her a couple of stories about his exploits as a sheriff and she had to give it to him – he seemed entirely suited to the job.

Rob kept somewhat to himself, remaining at the table while the others came and went to the dance floor. After a while, Autumn began to worry that someone who so obviously had an axe to grind shouldn't be drinking so much, so fast.

It was already past midnight when the topic of the wedding came up again.

"Who's going to be your maid of honor?" Rose asked. She had joined the party when they reached the bar. Autumn took her aside when she arrived and explained all about the practical joke, which Rose found hilarious. She promised to pass the word on to her friend to pass on to her cousin, and told Autumn she'd do her best to spread the truth around to take the heat off of Rob. Not that Autumn cared if Rob ever dated again, but she didn't like the anger she saw in him, or the direction it was aimed – at Ethan.

"My best friend, Becka. She's flying in on Wednesday to help me get all the last minute details finished up."

"There you go, Rob," Jamie said with a wink. "New blood. This Becka girl won't know anything about your wicked ways – she'll dance with you at Ethan's wedding."

"Maybe she will," Rob said, tossing back another drink. "Speaking of the wedding, who's going to be the best man?"

Conversation died down as the group's attention shifted to Ethan, who rubbed his jaw and looked a little uncomfortable. "Cab, Rob, Jamie – you've all been good friends to me over the years, so I hope you'll all stand up with me, but seeing as how Jamie's giving me the chance to keep the ranch and becoming my business partner, I thought it was only right to choose him to be my best man. Whattya say, Jamie? Will you do it?"

"Hell, yeah!" Jamie raised his glass. "To the groom!"

"Here, here!" Everyone clinked their glasses together except for Rob. He stood up unsteadily and waited for talk to die down.

"I might have known. Some friend you turned out to be, Ethan Cruz. You owe your present happiness to me and you know I could undo it in a minute if I cared to. Unlike you, I don't care to ruin my friends' love

178

lives. Just remember I can." He shoved his chair aside and stomped off across the bar, swaying a bit as he did so.

Autumn looked to Ethan in shock. "What does he mean?"

"You'd better go after him, Ethan, and smooth things over. Rob shouldn't drive like that," Claire said.

"Sorry, honey – I'll be right back. Claire's right – Rob's in a bad way and I don't want him behind the wheel."

Ethan rushed off after him, leaving Autumn in a circle of sympathetic and definitely uncomfortable faces. More than ever she wished she and Ethan had spent the night home alone.

Chapter Fourteen

An hour later, Ethan still hadn't caught up with Rob. By the time he made it to the parking lot, Rob's Chevy was long gone. He'd gone to Rob's house first, just to make sure his friend made it home okay, but to his surprise, Rob's truck wasn't among the other vehicles parked at the Matheson ranch and the cabin he lived in, a quarter mile from the main house, was empty and dark when he poked his head in the door. Numerous calls to his cell phone yielded no answer and he began to get worried.

Back in town, he searched two other bars and an all-night restaurant before heading to a dive on the county road. He couldn't imagine Rob hanging out there, but it was the only place left to try. Rob's truck wasn't in the lot, but he slammed on his brakes when he saw Lacey pull in and get unsteadily out of her car. He pulled into a parking spot nearby and intercepted her before she could reach the front door.

"Hey – Lacey, what are you doing? Are you meeting Carl?"

She made a face. "I left Carl at home and I came here because I didn't want to see any familiar faces.

What're you doing here – finally break up with that floozy?"

"No, I haven't broken up with Autumn. We're getting married on Saturday, remember? I'm just here looking for Rob."

"Rob?" She shrugged. "Haven't seen him. Come on, I'll buy you a drink."

"Sorry – I've got to go, and you should go, too. You're drunk, Lacey, and if you go in there some asshole is going to figure that out in about two seconds, get you drunker, and take you home. You don't want that kind of trouble."

"How the hell do you know what I want?" she hissed at him. "You walked away from me."

Ethan raised his eyebrows in disbelief. "I walked away? You gotta be kidding me. You left me, Lacey, remember?"

"You were supposed to fight for me!" she said, jabbing a finger into his chest. "You were supposed to man up, pay off those debts, come after me and give me what I wanted."

"Uh...you made it pretty damn clear you didn't want anything to do with me. Besides, you were with Carl – I'm not going to try to steal another man's woman."

"I'm not Carl's woman," she said, rearing back. "I'm not anyone's woman. No one loves me enough for me to be his woman."

"Carl loves you."

"Carl says I drink too much. Do you believe that?" Lacey said, "He said I need to get my act together before we get married. All because I had a little, tiny glass of wine with supper."

"Lacey, you've had way more than a glass of wine. Go home and sober up. Pull it together. You found a rich man who's willing to put up with all of your shit and make an honest woman of you – you should be happy."

"I'm not happy," she said and lurched forward into his arms. "Ethan, I'm not happy at all. Carl bores me to tears, he isn't any fun, and…" She flung her arms around him and kissed him squarely on the mouth. "I love you, Ethan. Not Carl. I'm in love with you."

He was going to have nightmares about this night for the rest of his life, he just knew it. He firmly removed Lacey's arms from around his neck and pushed her away. "No, you're not, Lacey. And I'm not in love with you, either."

"Yes, I am. And I know you still love me. You haven't forgotten my body, have you? You used to love to touch me – you couldn't wait to make love to me. Remember that picture you took of me sleeping in your bed – the one I put on your office wall so you would think about being with me even when you were working?"

Ethan sucked in a breath. Shit – he still hadn't taken that stupid collage down. He'd even gone looking for a scraper once while Autumn was busy, but had gotten distracted by Jamie coming to see him about ranch business.

Watching him closely, she crowed with triumph. "You still have it, don't you! You still look at my naked body every night when you do your accounts. You still dream about touching me. See – I knew you were still in love with me. You don't have to go through with the wedding, Ethan. You can break it off and marry me, instead. It'll be so beautiful…"

Ethan backed away. "You're crazy if you think for one second I'll have you back. Get it in your head – I love Autumn. I always will. Go home and sleep it off and see if Carl will still have you after whatever you've done to him tonight. Or better yet, figure out what you really want in life. Take a trip, or get a job, or go back to school or something. Stop trying to find a man to fill in all the blanks and start filling them in yourself."

He opened the door and stuck his head in the bar for a minute, to assure himself of what he already knew – Rob wasn't in there – then brushed Lacey aside and stalked off down the steps, back to his truck. As he pulled out of the parking lot, he saw her fumble in her purse and pull out her phone. He felt bad leaving Lacey standing there, but he had to find Rob and he couldn't very well give her a ride home – not without fending off more drunken advances. He hoped she was calling a cab, or better yet – Carl.

Now where the hell was Rob? He'd just have to keep driving up and down the streets of Chance Creek until he found the man.

Some celebration.

Autumn waved to Jamie and let herself into the dark, empty bunkhouse, flipping on the kitchen lights and pouring herself a glass of water before heading wearily to the guest bedroom. Ethan never returned to the Dancing Boot, even though she'd waited nearly an hour and a half for him. Finally, she'd accepted a ride home with Jamie and Claire, half-sick with worry, half-dead with exhaustion.

Who knew when Ethan would turn up? Maybe Rob was hurt, or needed someone to talk to. She hoped Ethan could soothe over the man's obviously hurt feelings and patch things up between them. She knew how important it was to him to have all his friends stand up for him at the wedding.

If he was going to have three attendants, she guessed she'd better get her sister to be a bridesmaid along with Becka. If she was coming. There had been complete silence on the Eastern front and she had no idea if her sister and mother would be there on Saturday or not.

Maybe this is all a big mistake, she thought, sitting down on the bed. *Maybe we're rushing things because we know deep down we shouldn't be doing it at all.*

Did she really feel that way?

No – she loved Ethan, she was sure of that. And she wanted to be here at the Cruz ranch. It was just this business with Rob that had her spooked. What did he mean Ethan wouldn't be marrying her if it wasn't for him?

When the house phone rang, she jumped, then put a hand to her pounding heart and raced to get it. "Ethan?"

"No, it's Lacey. Is this Autumn?"

Autumn looked at the phone. Why would Lacey be calling at this hour? "Yes."

"Ethan will be home soon, but I thought you'd want to know why he's so late."

"He's looking for Rob," Autumn said sharply, moving to hang up.

Lacey laughed. "Well, that's the excuse he'll use, but he's actually been with me."

"You're a lousy liar," Autumn said, but a little voice asked how Lacey knew he wasn't home with her.

"That may be, but I'm the one who's been making out with Ethan for the past hour, and you're the one sitting home alone."

She paced across the kitchen, her free hand balled into a fist. The clock read past two in the morning. Where was Ethan? Why wasn't he home?

"You know Ethan could never keep his hands off of me. We did it two, three times a day when we were together. Inside, outside, in his truck." Lacey broke off with a throaty laugh.

"Whatever. Lacey, you're past history. Go to bed."

"You want proof Ethan's still in love with me? Proof that he can't get my body out of his mind even now that I'm marrying Carl? He goes into his office every night after dinner, doesn't he? Know what he's doing? I bet he's never let you in there."

"What?" How did Lacey know she hadn't been in Ethan's office? There'd never been a reason for her to go in there and he always kept the door closed to hide the mess, or so he'd said. "He's doing the accounts," Autumn snapped, but a little tendril of dread tightened in her gut. She hated to think that Ethan's daily rituals were as familiar to Lacey as they were to her. More familiar, actually. Lacey had dated Ethan for months, right? Years, even. She'd only been with him for three weeks.

"Is that what he calls it?" Another throaty laugh. "Uh uh, darling. You see, he calls me every night. If I'm not in, he listens to my answering machine, and he looks at my photograph – my naked photograph – and…well, you can picture the rest."

"That is such bullshit," Autumn said.

"Is it? Check out his office. You'll see exactly what I mean. Oh, and by the way, that YouTube video – the one that lured you to Montana in the first place because you were so desperate for a husband? Ethan didn't even make it. Rob did. As a joke." Lacey hung up and Autumn stood there, nausea crawling up her throat, the phone still held in her hand.

Lacey couldn't be serious – about any of it. There was no way Ethan was getting off to her answering machine in his office every night and then coming out and making love to her with a passion that swept her off her feet. There was no way this whole thing was a joke.

But what if he *was* thinking of Lacey when he was with her?

No. No way could he fake that.

What if he was only with her because Lacey was marrying Carl?

She couldn't believe that, either.

And what did Lacey mean that Rob had made the YouTube video instead of Ethan? That couldn't be true – except…she remembered Rob's words at the restaurant: "Without me you'd never be marrying Autumn…"

The whole thing had been a joke?

She was a joke?

She placed the phone back in its cradle with trembling hands and slowly made her way to Ethan's bedroom, halting at the closed door to his office. She tentatively reached out and turned the handle. The door swung open, revealing a room so small the desk took up an entire wall.

She stepped in, turned on the light and cried out.

There on the wall beside his desk, just as Lacey had said, was a mass of photographs. All of them showed Lacey in various outfits at various locations, but smack in the middle of all of them was a very provocative, very naked image of Lacey. Right where Ethan would have to see it, every single night.

Tears filled her eyes and she flicked off the light. She backed out of the room, and blindly retraced her steps. He was still in love with Lacey – or in lust, or something. At the very least he spent nearly twenty minutes every night with her naked image before he was able to make love to her.

Shame burned the back of her throat and she stumbled to the guest bedroom and began to pack. She had to get out of here, right now. She was a pathetic stand-in for the woman Ethan truly loved and there was no way she'd spend her life as someone else's second choice.

And everyone knew. Everyone in the restaurant tonight – at the bar – they all knew. She recalled the tension at the table as they waited with bated breath to see whether or not Rob would spill Ethan's big secret – that the whole video ad for a mail order bride was a big, fat fake, and her wedding was probably a big, fat fake, too.

Wiping her face with the back of her hand, she pulled open the drawers of the bureau and began to pile her clothing on the bed. Was that it? Was the whole damn town in on the gag? When would Ethan have told her? At the altar? Before or after they exchanged their fake vows?

You were lying to him, too. If you'd submitted the article you came to write, all of New York City would be laughing at Ethan.

Tears spilled down over her cheeks. She bent to grab her suitcase and cursed when the lid swung open and a package fell out on her foot.

The pregnancy test.

Shit. Shit. Shit.

She sat down hard and covered her face with her hands as sobs wracked her. Ethan was supposed to be here. He was supposed to be as excited as she was to find out whether or not they were having a child, but instead he was who knows where, tangled up in a web of lies so thick he'd trapped her good and hard within them.

She wiped her eyes with her sleeve and stared at the box for a full minute before slowly retrieving it. She might as well do it now, so she knew exactly what type of hell she'd be returning to New York City to face.

Five minutes later she sat on the closed lid of the toilet and stared at the plus sign on the pregnancy test stick.

Pregnant. She was carrying Ethan's child. A few hours ago she would have been deliriously happy to see what she was seeing now, and she'd have bet her life Ethan would be happy, too. Now fear, disgust, and self-loathing gathered in her chest, crushing her. Not only would she be alone; her baby would be, too. She would do whatever it took to give this baby a good life, but just like her mother before her she needed to return to school, ask for help from her family, and leave the baby in the care of strangers while she took classes and found a better job. She would miss so many experiences with her child because she would need to be a breadwinner. And what about Ethan? What place would he demand in her child's life? For all she hated him right now – for all he'd possessed her heart and then torn it into pieces – she couldn't deny him his rights as a father.

Would he want to be involved? Or would he just move on and have children with Lacey?

Finally, when her heart hurt too much to bear it anymore, she returned to the guest room and shoved the pregnancy test into her bag. As evidence, she guessed. Evidence that she was the biggest idiot in Montana for believing this life could ever be hers.

When her bags were packed she sat on the bed and waited for Ethan to come home. As soon as she told him exactly what she thought of him, she was getting the hell out of Chance Creek for good.

Chapter Fifteen

Ethan opened the back door as quietly as possible, in case Autumn was already asleep. He never did find Rob, but Cab – with the help of his buddies in the sheriff's department – finally got a lead that he'd been spotted in Billings. Cab would make sure he stayed out of trouble for the rest of the night and got home safely.

All he wanted was to curl up with his bride and sleep – unless she had other ideas, that is. Autumn could wake up his passion with a single touch – hell, even a single look – and he'd never disappoint her. The kitchen light was on, but she wasn't in sight. Nor was she in his bedroom, which gave him pause until he saw the light on in the guest room. Why would she be in there? He moved softly to the door and pushed it open.

Autumn was awake, fully dressed and sitting upright on the made bed, her suitcases at her feet.

"Don't say a thing," she said as he entered the room, and her tone made his blood run cold.

"Autumn…"

"Not one thing." Her voice rose and he held up his hands in an appeasing gesture. "I talked to Lacey tonight," she went on. "She had a lot of interesting things to say."

Ethan groaned. "I'll bet she did. You know that woman's crazier than a loon, don't you?"

"Did you kiss her tonight?"

Ethan's mouth dropped open, closed, then opened again. "She...I didn't kiss her."

Autumn closed her eyes and he wanted to rush to her and smooth away every trace of the pain that was evident in her face.

"Autumn, I swear, I didn't kiss her. She's the one that threw herself at me. She was drunk and upset – something must have happened between her and Carl, I don't know what. I got out of there as quickly as I could and I came back here."

Her eyes snapped open. "She called me over an hour ago."

"I've been looking for Rob! You know that. Hell, don't let Lacey screw this up between us – not now," Ethan pleaded. "That woman's been nothing but trouble since I met her. She's long gone, Autumn. Past history – she's got no part in our story."

Autumn said nothing, getting to her feet. Her eyes were shining with tears and a jagged pain stabbed through Ethan's heart knowing he was the cause of it. "That woman is on your office wall. Naked on your office wall."

Oh, hell.

Oh, holy hell.

"I can explain." The words sounded so lame he wanted to gouge his own eyes out.

"No, you can't." She sounded tired. "Ethan, please. Don't even try – it doesn't become either of us."

"It was so long ago – Lacey put them there when we started fighting, before we split up, and she used some kind of glue. I don't know how she did it. They won't peel off – I need to find a scraper and some solvent...and there's always too damn much to do out there," he waved a hand toward the ranch. "At first, when she ditched me, I kept it up because I was furious. She hurt my pride, telling me I was broke and worthless and she deserved better than me. She left a month after my parents died. You don't know how I felt. Every time I saw that picture I remembered again how she'd done me wrong. It kept me feeling angry – and feeling angry felt better than feeling alone. Then I just got busy, and I didn't care, and I stopped seeing it there all together. It's just part of the room – like the desk or the window. I'll take care of it tomorrow – I'll do it right now if you need me to."

She shook her head. "You didn't even make the YouTube video. You didn't even want a wife. It's all a joke – this is all a joke. We both know you still love Lacey."

"Fuck and hell, if you believe that then you're the one who's crazy!" Autumn's eyes went wide at the anger in his voice, but he stepped forward, needed to drive his point home. "I love you. I have loved you from the minute I saw you walk through the airport and I want you to be my wife. Do you understand that?" She blinked and a tear spilled from her eye. "I made a mistake proposing to Lacey and thank God she broke it off, because if we'd gone through with marriage we would have made each other very miserable." He took her arm, gently but firmly. "I may not have made that video, but God must have moved Rob's hand to do it, because it brought me an angel – you. I've been a lucky man. I was saved from an unhappy marriage before it was too late, and then I was led to you – the woman I love more than anything. Taking down those pictures was a chore that required just a bit too much time and effort to make it to the top of my list. I will regret that little bit of laziness forever since it hurt you.

"I'm just a man, Autumn. A flawed man. But I love you more than you will ever know."

"She said you called her every night," Autumn whispered. "She said you looked at her photo and…"

Ethan counted to ten. The next time he saw Lacey it would be all he could do to keep from ripping her head right off her body. "That's a lie, and I can prove it. I'll get my phone records tomorrow – both the house and my cell. I'll show you I haven't spoken to Lacey since she dumped me."

"Why would she lie?"

He shook his head. Should he explain all he knew about Lacey? Expose her secrets? "Lacey…I don't know. Why does any woman lie?"

"Men lie, too," Autumn blazed back.

"Not all men."

"My father cheated on my mother. He left her for another woman – left her with two daughters to raise. He changed all of our lives in that moment, in ways I'm sure he never even considered. My mom was never the same." Her voice broke. "He disappeared, so I never got to tell him what he did. He made her hate men and he made her so scared for her daughters that she did everything she could to make us hate men, too. And I've tried," her voice rose. "I've tried to care about work, heart and soul like she does. I've tried to be a success, and to put everything else aside. Before you, I'd never once considered marriage or having children and you know what?"

"What?" He was afraid to say anything else.

"It's lonely. I go home every night from my job and open the door to my empty apartment, where I can't even keep a cat if I want to, and I work some more or watch t.v., or maybe go out with a friend, but even if there are men there I keep my distance because I. can't. trust. a. man. I can't! Because my mother raised me never to do so. And then I come here – here! – to your ranch," she waved an arm, her eyes brimming with the tears she was struggling not to shed, "and here you were, and here was this place, and here was the life I wanted, and I thought maybe I could trust a man…and…I was so happy…and then Lacey called…"

Ethan spun away before she saw the fury in his eyes. Lacey was going to pay – he'd make sure of that. "You're not the only one here who's been hurt. Hell, everyone gets hurt, don't they?" He turned back around. "All we can do is try. And if you love me half as much as I love you, I think we have a good shot at making it."

Autumn hesitated, her eyes huge and her cheeks stained with tears. "I want us to make it."

"I want that, too." In an instant he had her in his arms, and tipping her head back he kissed her long and hard. At first she resisted and he knew she was thinking of Lacey's picture in the office. Hell, he'd burn the whole house down if that's what it took to put that in their past. Then she softened and he took the kiss deeper, until his body woke up enough to think they should get on to even more pleasurable activities.

"Ethan," she said, when he reached for the buttons at her throat. "Wait."

He stilled, afraid she would push him away again.

"Do you really love me?"

"I love you more than life itself."

A tiny smile appeared on her face. He thought it was the most beautiful thing he'd ever seen.

"Are you sure you want to spend your life with me?"

"So sure, honey. Nothing could make me happier."

She waited another beat. "I'm pregnant."

He went cold and then hot and then tears pricked his eyes – tears – when he hadn't cried in nearly twenty years, not even when his parents died. "Are you sure?"

She nodded vehemently and he pulled her into a hug and spun her around the room. Collapsing with her onto the bed he kissed her thoroughly on the mouth, and then all over her body, stopping with reverence at her still-flat stomach. "Hey, baby," he called, cupping his hands over her belly. "I love you. I can't wait to see you."

When he looked up, Autumn was in tears, too.

"I love you, Ethan," she said.

"I love you. Six more days until the wedding, and then I'm never letting you go – ever again."

Chapter Sixteen

By Wednesday, Lacey's pictures were long gone, replaced by a bare, scrubbed space on the wall that Ethan dubbed the *Idiot Reminder*.

"From now on any time I put off a chore I'm going to see that mark and get right to it," he said.

Autumn laughed and was overjoyed that she could laugh about it. Once she got over the shock of the incident and heard the whole story, she had to admit it was kind of funny. Not very funny, mind you, but mildly so.

"I'd rather you just forget all about it," she said to Ethan.

"I've already forgotten everything but you."

That afternoon they drove to the airport to pick up Becka. She was excited to see her best friend – it seemed so long since she'd left New York – and show her all around the ranch. Inside, the terminal was crowded and it felt like they waited forever before passengers from Becka's plane finally came down the corridor. Autumn bounced when she spotted her friend's fire-red hair, and pushed through the crowd to meet her.

"Becka, you made it! Thank goodness you're here – I need you!"

"Before you get too excited, I've got a surprise for you," Becka said and pulled away. She turned and gestured behind her, and only then did Autumn see her mother and sister waiting there.

"Mom!" Autumn rushed to her mother, then stopped, unsure.

"Come here," Teresa said and pulled her into a stiff hug. "You honestly didn't think I'd skip my daughter's wedding, did you? Even if it did come out of the blue and is happening much too fast?"

"I wasn't sure," Autumn said into the fabric of her mother's shirt. She felt the tension in her mother's stance and knew it would take time to smooth this over. "I hoped you'd come." She pulled back.

"Of course I came." Teresa looked at Ethan. "And you are the cowboy I've heard about. Swept my daughter right off her feet with your fancy hat and shiny spurs?"

"Mom!" Autumn flushed to the roots of her hair but Ethan laughed.

"That's me. Don't worry, Mrs. Leeds – your daughter is in good hands."

"Hmph. That's Teresa to you. Don't you dare call me Mom."

"I can't believe you're getting married!" Lily said and gave her a big hug. "You're not even thirty!" She whispered into Autumn's ear, "Good for you."

Autumn hugged her tight. "Come on – I can't wait for you to see the ranch."

If she thought she was busy before, now that her family had arrived she felt like she'd been swept up in a whirlpool of activity. She spent Thursday picking out bridesmaid gowns with Becka and her sister, elegant pale mint sheaths that contrasted well both with Becka's red hair and her sister's darker locks. Her mother surprised her by offering to pay for the dresses and even to reimburse Autumn for the cost of her gown. Although Autumn declined at first, she was secretly relieved since her dress, although cheap by New York City standards, had taken up a large chunk of the available balance on her credit card. Rose had ended up being a huge help with other aspects of the ceremony. She arranged for several women in town to pitch in to provide floral arrangements from their gardens, and organized a pot luck reception, aside from the barbecued steaks that would come from the ranch's own beef. Ethan hired a local band for the reception and while Ethan told her Rob swore he'd hired a chapel ahead of time for the wedding, that turned out to be another joke. Both wedding and reception would occur at the ranch, on the wide front lawn with a backdrop of the mountains.

"Photographer?" Becka blurted suddenly when they were making a light dinner. It was the first time Autumn had cooked in the Big House and she couldn't tear her eyes from the view out the huge windows.

Becka and her family had taken over several of the bedrooms upstairs, so it made sense for them all to eat here rather than crowd around the small table in the bunkhouse.

"Rose's friend Alice is doing it in exchange for being able to use some of the photos in her portfolio."

"Rings?"

"Yep."

"Bouquet – wait, Rose has that covered."

"That's right."

Becka tapped her finger on the granite countertop. "Party favors?"

Autumn frowned. "Do we really need those?"

"Yes, you do, and don't worry – I'll take care of it tomorrow. They can be really simple and I want to contribute something."

A wave of nervousness swept over Autumn and she dropped the knife she was holding and gripped the edge of the countertop. "I can't do this."

Becka laughed. "Yes, you can."

"What if it's all wrong? What if he hates me the next day or the guest ranch flops or he hates the baby?"

"Ethan's not going to hate the baby," Becka laughed. "For heaven's sake, Autumn – you're fine. It's all going to be fine! Ethan worships the ground you walk on and that baby is going to wrap him around its little finger, whether it's a girl or a boy. Now shush or your mom will hear us. Seriously, honey – you're just having wedding jitters."

She smiled, but Autumn knew this went beyond wedding jitters. She still hadn't told Ethan why she'd really come to Chance Creek. She'd already called her editor and told her she wasn't coming back to CityPretty. Margaret had been furious, of course, but had calmed down when she said she didn't expect to be paid for any of her time since she'd left New York. She'd given notice on her apartment, as well. She had to fly back for a couple of days and pack up her things, but otherwise her life in New York was over. Should she tell Ethan the truth or just let it slip away, too? Why rock the boat now when everything was going so well?

Because Ethan deserves the truth.

She pushed away that thought. The truth would only hurt him. "Okay, you're right. I'm sure it will be fine."

But she wasn't sure. The last time she'd been so happy was just before her father walked out on her mother. How could she be sure fate wouldn't yank the carpet out from under her again?

Finally, he was alone with Autumn. Ethan buttoned his shirt and tucked it in hurriedly, then crossed the room to his bride and pulled her into his arms. She came willingly, and wrapped her arms around his neck, meeting his kiss with a fervor that matched his.

"When are you going to send those people away?" he growled into her neck.

"If by 'those people' you mean my best friend, my mother and my sister, I was thinking of inviting them along for the honeymoon," she said and then shrieked when he swatted her bottom. "They'll go home Sunday morning, but we'll be long gone by then."

Ethan's friends had pitched in and offered to take on Ethan's chores for a few days so they could have a small honeymoon in the Black Hills of South Dakota. It wasn't much to offer his new bride, but they'd be alone – away from the workaday cares of running a large spread and planning a new business. When they returned they'd get right to work on opening the Big House for guests.

"I can't wait. I've got a lot of ideas of how we can spend the time away, and very few of them have to do with sightseeing."

"That's okay by me." Autumn snuggled into his embrace. "I'm so happy, I just can't believe it. I keep thinking something's going to happen to spoil it."

Was that genuine worry in her voice? "Nothing will spoil this. I promise. We're going to be this happy for the rest of our lives." He bent down and kissed her again, until the only thing he could think of was getting her back out of these clothes and into bed, but Autumn finally pushed him away.

"We've got to go – everyone will be waiting for us."

Tonight was the rehearsal dinner. One more hurdle to clear before he could be alone with his bride on their honeymoon. In twenty-four hours they would be husband and wife. By the look in Autumn's eyes, she was thinking along the same lines.

"I can't wait to be married to you," she said.

"Neither can I."

Sage was the fanciest restaurant in town, but Autumn would much rather be at DelMonaco's. In fact, Becka, her mother and sister were the only ones who looked at home in the fine dining establishment. Teresa was the one who insisted they eat there. The rest of the party were picking at their food – especially Cab, who looked at the bite sized filet mignon on his plate with something akin to desperation.

Conversation was a little stilted as well. Becka did her best to fill in the gaps, asking the men many questions about their jobs, and Autumn learned that Rob – still sullen that he wasn't the best man, but in slightly better spirits since Ethan brought him a bottle of whiskey to smooth things over – loved ranching but loved the rodeo more, Cab won all kinds of pistol competitions but had never shot a man in the line of duty, and Jamie was considered something of a horse-whisperer in this part of the world. Cab questioned her mother and sister about their lines of work, but doctoring – especially gynecology – doesn't make good mealtime conversation, and the talk soon died down again.

The waitress, a young blonde with her hair pulled back in a severe bun wearing an all black uniform, had just begun to clear the plates when a commotion toward the entrance of the restaurant caught everyone's attention.

Lacey swept into the room and Autumn's heart plummeted. This was what she'd been dreading – another scene with the woman who seemed determined to ruin her happiness.

What was that under her arm?

Oh my god – it couldn't be.

It was.

"Lacey, get out of here," Cab said, standing up and trying to intercept her. Lacey ducked around him and high-tailed it to Ethan. Her high heels clicked on the hardwood floor and she was dressed elegantly enough to fit right in here at the restaurant – far better than half the guests at the table, Autumn thought a trifle hysterically.

She dropped Autumn's laptop with a clatter on top of Ethan's dinner plate, opened it and pressed the power button.

"So sorry to spoil your meal," she said. "But I had to come and show you just exactly how your lying bitch of a fiancée is playing you for a fool!"

"Lacey – get out of here. This is low even for you." Ethan stood up and grabbed her forearm, trying to muscle her away from the table. She pushed past him again and jabbed at the keyboard.

"Recognize this? It's your fiancee's." She straightened to stare him down. "When you popped up with her at DelMonaco's that night I thought you were pulling my leg – that you'd just picked up some passing tourist at a bar and brought her to dinner to get my goat. When I heard you two got really drunk and nearly got it on in Rob's truck, I thought maybe you hired a hooker to play the part. Then I heard you were living together and I didn't know what to think anymore. I finally weaseled the truth out of Rob about the YouTube video."

Autumn turned to look at Rob, along with everyone else at the table. Becka and her family were pale with shock. Cab was fighting to get around the crowded table to Lacey. Rob crossed his arms defensively, meeting the combined gazes of the group, but Autumn thought he looked guilty. "Hell, I was drunk. I didn't mean to spill the beans."

So that's how Lacey knew about the video, Autumn thought.

"I tried to scare her off for you, Ethan, but she didn't scare," Lacey said. Did she really think that pouting, baby-doll look was going to lure Ethan away less than 24 hours before his wedding day? This went beyond jealousy, Autumn thought. Maybe Lacey was mentally ill.

"You told her we were having an affair," Ethan said. "That's messed up."

She thinned her lips in a tight smile. "I did what I thought was best and you're going to thank me for it when you see what I found on her computer. She's been lying to you all along, Ethan! Haven't you ever wondered why a woman like her would answer a damn YouTube video? Look at her - the minute I saw

Autumn I knew she was hiding something. She's a knockout – a city girl. And she's not stupid – anyone can see that. So why would she respond to a video made a by a drunk-ass cowboy? Why get engaged to someone sight-unseen? I figured right from the start either she was crazy, in trouble, or running some scam of her own. And I was right." She swung the laptop to face him. "Did you guys not do any kind of research on her?"

Ethan gaped at her and Autumn's heart sunk. Lacey must have found the notes she'd written for the story the first few nights she was in town. She jumped to her feet and lunged for the computer, but Lacey snatched it out of her grasp.

"See? She doesn't want you to see, because she knows exactly what I'm going to show you. She's a total faker, Ethan. How could you not even do a search on her name?"

"I hate computers – you know that!"

Autumn didn't know whether to laugh or cry. She saw her wedding slipping away – her life with Ethan slipping away. She felt like she was trapped in a nightmare and she didn't know how to wake up before she lost everything she held dear.

"Autumn's a writer, Ethan. For CityPretty – one of the hottest, sleaziest women's magazines out there.

"Who cares? She quit when she came out here," Ethan sputtered, and looked to her. "Right, Autumn? You quit before you met me?"

Autumn stared back, tears filling her eyes. She'd always deflected questions about her former life. They talked about him – the ranch, the money problems, his family, the garden, their future plans. He'd assumed she'd tied up any loose ends from her past life and she'd let him think that.

"No, Ethan. She didn't quit. She writes feature pieces for them. If you read them, you'd know she's not the sweet little thing she's pretending to be. She's a total bitch. Want to know what she's working on right now?"

He kept staring at Autumn and nausea grew within her until she pressed a hand to her throat. She would never live through this, let alone salvage her relationship with Ethan. She was going to die right now. "What?" he asked, his voice thin.

"How I Became an E-Mail Order Bride. I don't think it's catchy enough – you'd better work on that, Autumn." Lacey shot her a look both malicious and triumphant. "She's got lots of notes. Tons of photographs to go with the article – I bet she gets paid double for supplying the images, too. Pretty savvy girl you got there. You look mighty hot, cowboy."

Autumn swallowed hard as Ethan finally tore his gaze from hers and reached for the laptop.

This was it.

She'd lost him for good.

Chapter Seventeen

Ethan tried to shake off the creeping darkness that fringed his vision as he scrolled through the pages of Autumn's notes. "Shit." His chest felt tight and it was hard to breathe. It was all a lie? Autumn had been lying to him?

In her notes, she wrote about making her video – all the tricks she and Becka – Becka? He glanced up at the girl, who wouldn't meet his gaze – had used to make her supremely attractive to the cowboy who'd put up the wife-wanted video. She described the plane ride to Montana, her first glimpse of him and his friends at the airport – the swirl of raw testosterone in the air that caused her heart to pound.

Yeah, right.

The notes went on and on. The dinner at DelMonaco's – after his lame attempt to get take out food instead. Getting it on in Rob's truck and then finishing at the bunkhouse. Taking a picnic lunch to him on the range at the suggestion of his creepy neighbor, Rob – the one who liked to lure women home to make porno flicks.

Jesus.

Lacey was right – incisive, snarky. Autumn hit every nerve a guy could have until he felt like he'd been flayed alive. And she was going to publish this?

"Ethan – it's not what it looks like."

He glanced up and met Autumn's beseeching gaze. Her eyes were shining with tears, a trick she used all too often, he realized now.

"Looks pretty clear cut to me," he ground out, hardly recognizing his own voice.

"I don't understand, Autumn. Who is this? What's happening?" Teresa waved at Lacey who still hung over Ethan's shoulder.

"What's happening is your daughter faked this whole thing," Lacey said, her face alight with a vicious triumph. "Your daughter needed a subject for an article. She answered a want ad for a wife, came out here and fooled Ethan into thinking she'd really marry him and instead she planned to take off just before the wedding and write an expose about the whole thing. She was going to roast him in front of the whole nation – a big, fat joke – a stupid cowboy who wanted a wife and got duped instead. Of course, she didn't realize she was the stupid one – the whole ad was a fake."

Teresa shook her head. "Autumn? What's going on?"

"Mrs. Leeds," Ethan scraped back his chair and rose to his full height. "What's going on is the wedding is off. Your daughter and I are done. I don't know if you are in on it or not and at this point I don't give a damn. Collect your things, get out of my house and get the hell out of Montana. All of you!"

His heart nearly gave out when he saw Autumn's face. Pale as a sheet, stricken, desolation writ large in her eyes. Those lying, scheming, cheating eyes.

She probably had a boyfriend back home – some metrosexual guy who didn't give a damn if his girl slept with a cowboy as long as she brought home a good story to tell. And made a few bucks off of publishing the story. God damn it all to hell.

He slammed through the restaurant, shaking Jamie off when the man caught up with him.

"Ethan, I'm driving. You can't get behind the wheel like this."

"The hell I can't!"

"I'm not going to let you. Give me the keys. Now!"

Jamie was right, he could hardly see through the haze of red in front of his eyes, let alone navigate a highway without killing someone. He wanted to kill someone, though. He wanted to rip someone to shreds.

Instead, he allowed Jamie to push him toward the passenger seat and soon they were out on the highway, cruising as fast as the speed limit would let them.

He was thankful the man kept his mouth shut. The last thing he needed right now was pity. Or advice.

Ten minutes passed before Jamie opened his mouth. "You know that's Lacey back there, showing you those files. You didn't even ask Autumn if it was true."

"It's true." He'd seen it in Autumn's eyes.

"There might be an explanation."

"Doubt it." He knew enough of the world to know people did things for several basic reasons. Greed. Desire. Or hate. Greed in this case.

"Autumn deserves a chance to give her side."

"Does she?" They rode in silence for several minutes. "Shit." His head bowed under the crushing weight of all his dreams collapsing on him.

"What?"

"Autumn's pregnant." Or at least he thought she was. Had she faked that, too? Could you fake a pregnancy test? "I think." He met Jamie's brief, pitying gaze. "I don't know."

Jamie slowed the truck and pulled to the side of the highway. "I don't think you can run from this one, Ethan. It's fucked up every which way from Sunday, but you need to see it through. Things weren't right on your side at the beginning, either, remember? The ad was a joke and by all rights we should have sent Autumn home on the next flight when she landed at the airport, but you didn't because you were attracted to her and you wanted to see how things turned out. You fell in love with her over time and changed your mind about the joke." Jamie shrugged. "The joke became real. What if it's the same way for Autumn?"

Ethan felt a pang of guilt. Jamie was right, he hadn't been truthful with Autumn, either. "What do you mean?"

"What if she answered the ad as a joke – as a funny way to write an article? Then, when she came out here she fell in love with you and decided to make the marriage work. She got pregnant, she's been sleeping with you for weeks, right? Hell, she figured out how to save the ranch and got the two of us to be business partners!"

"That could all be for the story."

"Sure, it could be. But is it? How far did those notes of hers go?"

Ethan tried to think back. There was the picnic, getting the ring…and hardly anything after that. She'd stopped writing about their relationship and she hadn't even downloaded any more pictures.

"The first couple of days, I guess."

"See?" Jamie leaned forward. "Just like you – it started out fake and then turned real. Shouldn't you at least give her a chance to say something?"

Ethan leaned back in the seat and stared at the ceiling. "I don't know."

"I do." Jamie started the engine and spun the wheel around.

Chapter Eighteen

Autumn faced the people grouped around the table, feeling like she'd been suddenly stripped in public and made to confess her deepest sins. Becka was pale and wide-eyed, her sister confused and alarmed. Her mother was steely-eyed and Autumn dreaded that conversation the most. Teresa hated lies and would not abide a daughter who could perpetrate a scam like this, even if she had fallen in love for real and given up any idea of writing the article weeks ago.

Rob got to his feet. "Autumn – I'm sorry. I shouldn't have said anything."

Lacey slammed her fist down on the table so hard the silverware jumped. "Of course you should have said something! You want Ethan to marry a lying whore? What kind of woman does something like this?" She pointed to the words and photos still visible on the laptop screen.

Autumn cringed. Why had she done it? What was wrong with her that she'd ever considered taking on such a story? She'd proceeded from such stupid assumptions – that a man who advertised for a wife was an idiot. That cowboys in general were ignorant –

ripe for exploitation. She thought of how she and Becka had laughed until they cried milking every stereotype while they made her video – how she'd considered it perfectly acceptable to have a fling with a man who stated up front he was seeking a wife, and then go home and write about it. She'd been subverting her values for years in order to reach some kind of success, and what did she have to show for it?

Hell, CityPretty magazine as a whole was an exercise in exploitation. If she wasn't skewering someone or something for her readers' benefit, she was writing articles calculated to leave them dissatisfied with their lives or worse. The day she called her editor and quit was one of the happiest of her life. She hadn't realized what a strain it was to work there until she'd felt the relief of letting the job go.

She'd been a jackal, making a living off other people's unhappiness.

And Lacey was right – she'd been a whore.

She'd come out here and practically spread her legs for the story. Yes, she was attracted to Ethan – more than she'd ever been attracted to any other man – but she slept with him without knowing him, without understanding the pressures his own life put upon him. She'd gambled with his heart.

She'd gambled with a child's life.

Because she had worked to humiliate the father of this child just so she could make a buck, even if she'd changed her mind and called the article off. And now, this child would grow up with a father who hated its mother. Nausea soured her mouth and she stood up, unsteady on trembling legs. She had no job to support the baby. She'd have to beg her mother for help, move back home.

Was it fair to live 2,000 miles from the baby's father? What about visitations?

Would paying child support be the straw that broke Ethan's back?

No wonder Ethan had run from the restaurant – she thought her own heart would break it hurt so bad. All she knew was that she had to get out of here as fast as she could. She had to get home – to New York. She would fall on her mother's mercy, go back to school, get a real job – a high paying job.

She'd get a nanny to raise her child. And she wouldn't take a dime from Ethan. In fact, she'd help pay off his debts, too. Their baby deserved a chance to learn to ride a horse, to help Ethan fix fences and care for the livestock. To one day stand beside Ethan and survey land that had been in the Cruz family for generations.

Would the child hate her for what she'd done? Would she be left all alone in New York as her son or daughter fell in love with the ranch and chose their father over her?

Blind with tears now, her arms already aching for the loss of a child she had yet to hold, she pushed away from the table, first stumbling, then running as fast as she could. She found the ladies' room just as the heaving ache in her belly overwhelmed her, and she fell to her knees in a stall gasping, then was sick until her stomach was empty and she could be sick no more.

"Hey, Cowboy – you all right?"

When they reached the restaurant again, Lacey was the only one left at the table. She was nursing a shot of something, and looked tired.

Lacey. Figured. Ethan braced for the onslaught.

But she just played with the enormous ring on her finger. Would she take it off and declare herself free for the taking? Would she throw herself into his arms again?

He didn't give a shit. Even with Autumn gone his answer was still no. Thank God his parents weren't alive to see the mess he'd made out of his life. What would Claire say? By tomorrow everyone in town would know exactly the kind of idiot he was. Good luck finding a wife now.

"Have a seat. I'll order you some coffee." Lacey waved at a passing waitress. "Coffee, please?" The waitress looked at Jamie, who still hovered in the background. "None for him; he's just leaving."

"I'm leaving, too," Ethan said.

"I know you are," Lacey said, looking up at him at last. "But first you're going to give me the courtesy of five minutes of your time. Can you do that?"

He hesitated, not knowing why he didn't walk away. Something was different about Lacey, and he decided to hear her out. "It's okay, Jamie. Why don't you head on home. I can take it from here."

"You sure?"

Ethan nodded.

"All right. Call me if you need anything – I'll be back at the ranch."

"I'll be there soon."

The waitress came back with his coffee and he gripped the cup thankfully. Maybe it would help clear his mind.

Lacey shook her head. "I thought I had it all figured out," she said. "Even back in high school, I thought I'd graduate, marry you and everything would fall into place – I'd finally feel like I belonged somewhere – that I'd be worth something."

Ethan frowned. This kind of introspection wasn't normal for Lacey.

"I used to write our names over and over – Ethan and Lacey Cruz. I couldn't wait to stop being a Taylor."

Ethan nodded. He understood this. "I know things were rough at your place," he said quietly. Lacey's father had been a real piece of work when he was alive, heavy with the strap when his kids disappointed him. Lacey's older brothers lit out for Billings as soon as they could. Lacey stayed with her mother until she hooked up with Ethan, then with Carl.

"You don't know the half of it." Lacey laughed, but the sound wasn't pleasant. "I wish I'd been a boy. I could have stood the beatings. What he did..." she trailed off and Ethan's chest tightened.

218

"Hell, Lacey, did he…?" He couldn't say the words.

She nodded.

Oh, hell. "Why didn't you ever say?"

"So you could look at me that way? All pity and disgust?" A tear slid down her cheek and Ethan reached for her, but she pulled away. "No, I know you don't love me. And I don't really love you, either. I just couldn't stand that you and Autumn were going to be happy when I felt so…awful." Ethan moved toward her again and she held up a hand to stop him. "Look, you can't help me with this – I see that now – but I know I need help."

He waited for more, but she didn't speak.

"What made you see that?" he asked softly.

"This," she said, turning Autumn's laptop toward him. "I missed it the first time. You should be sure to read it. I've never loved anyone the way she loves you, and I finally get why – it's because I hate myself too much."

"Can I call Carl for you?" There was no way he was letting Lacey walk out of the restaurant alone. Not tonight.

"No – I can't lean on him anymore than I could lean on you. I've got to try another way. Rose is coming to get me."

Ethan took a breath. He sure as hell hadn't seen this coming. "Everything will be okay, Lacey. I know it," he said as she stood up.

"Well, that makes one of us." Her eyes were bright with tears, and his heart ached for her. "There's Rose. I guess I'd better get out of here before I make a bigger fool out of myself."

"You're no fool, Lacey Taylor. You'll do okay."

She nodded and hurried away. He watched her leave, then sat back down heavily. How could he have missed something so big? He'd spent years with Lacey and she'd never hinted at that kind of trouble at home. He knew one thing, though – if Lacey's father were alive, he'd beat him within an inch of his life. What kind of monster did that to his own daughter?

He reached for Autumn's laptop reluctantly, wondering what Lacey had seen there that changed her mind about love so completely. A document was displayed on the screen and he began to read.

"Today I fell in love with a man and my whole life has changed. I've been attracted to Ethan since the moment I got off the plane. Everything about him pushes all the right buttons – I've never had such an urge to tear off my clothes and jump into a man's arms. I love this feeling – like one minute with him can wash away every care in the world. To hell with writing an article – I'm going to write a love story, instead – between me and Ethan. The man I worship. The man I'll spend the rest of my life with."

Ethan didn't bother to read another line.

Autumn loved him and he wasn't going to waste another minute apart from her.

Chapter Nineteen

Autumn sat at the large dining room table in the great room of the Big House and watched Lily drag a suitcase down the stairway to the front hall. The door opened and Becka walked in with Autumn's luggage. Her friend had volunteered to do her packing so she wouldn't have to return to the bunkhouse and be reminded of her time there.

She had blurted out the whole story to her mother and sister on the awful ride home from the restaurant. Teresa guessed about her pregnancy instantly and demanded to be told the rest. As she'd predicted, her mother was coldly furious, her sister subdued.

She took a sip of the tea Becka had made her earlier. It was cold, but she didn't care. She didn't think anything would ever comfort her again. She'd lost Ethan for good. He must hate her guts. She didn't like herself much right now.

Lily crossed the room and sat down next to her. "Did you really come here to write a magazine article about Ethan?"

Her stomach contracted, but she knew she'd already thrown up everything it contained. "Yes. At least at first."

"What were you thinking?"

The condemnation in her voice sent Autumn over the edge. "I wasn't thinking, all right? I haven't...thought...in months! I've been terrified – I was about to lose my job. I could barely afford my apartment as it was. No matter what I do, I just screw it up!" To her horror, she began to cry again. How could she have any more tears left? "I saw Ethan's video – and it seemed perfect for a story. I didn't think it would work but I had to try. And then he chose me, and I came out here...I didn't think I'd fall in love with him!"

Lily didn't say anything and she scraped at her tears with the back of her hand. "I'm so stupid; I thought he loved me back, too. I was going to go through with it – marry him. Help him save the ranch. Have his baby."

"You mean you weren't going to publish the story?"

"No, of course not! It's a stupid story – the whole damn magazine is stupid! The whole damn city is stupid! I want this. I want...Ethan."

God, she must look a mess. Eyes dripping, nose running. But who cared? She'd lost everything she loved and her future spread before her as bleak as a moonscape and far less interesting. She didn't know how she'd get through the rest of the day, let alone the rest of her life. When she got back to New York she needed to totally reconstruct her life.

She dropped her head in her arms.

"Lily – would you go give your mom a hand? I don't think she should carry her suitcase down the stairs," Becka said, coming up behind Autumn and stroking her back.

"Are you kidding? Mom's as strong as a horse!" Lily said, but Becka must have shot her a look because Autumn heard her sister's footsteps fade away as she headed upstairs.

"Thanks," she whispered. Becka patted her.

"I know this is tough, honey, but you'll be all right."

"I don't think so."

"Yes, you will – you're a fighter. My money's on you, kid."

Autumn stood up and gave her friend a hug. "Thank God you're here. I couldn't do this without you."

"I'll always be here to help," Becka said, hugging her back.

"Hey – that's my fiancée you're pawing," a very masculine, very sexy voice drawled from the front door.

Becka started, then laughed nervously. "Well, what can I say – with you out of the picture I thought I'd give it a whirl..." She broke off and stepped away from Autumn.

Autumn raised her head. "Ethan?" Was he...joking around...with Becka? Her breath hitched as Ethan crossed to her and in one strong motion, swept her into her arms.

"I read what you wrote – Lacey showed me the part where you changed your mind. You weren't going to publish it." He kissed her soundly on the mouth.

Autumn's knees went weak and she clung to his arms. She couldn't breathe, tears already clogged her throat. Was this real? Was this Ethan – kissing her? After all that had happened?

"Of course not," she said. "I fell in love with you. I couldn't do that to my husband."

"I'm sorry I didn't let you explain."

"I'm sorry I ever planned to write it."

"I'm sorry I didn't tell you the video was a joke."

"I'm sorry..." No, she wasn't sorry for anything. She didn't care how they got here. All she cared about was being in Ethan's arms, holding him tight and kissing him over and over again.

"No more apologies," he growled. "If you hadn't planned to write it, you'd never have come, and I couldn't bear that."

"I couldn't bear it either."

He pulled away from her. "You know marriage is forever with me. Once you walk down that aisle tomorrow, there's no going back?" He searched her face. "I mean that, Autumn. Once you say yes, you say yes forever."

"Yes!" she said, tugging him closer for another kiss. "Yes! Yes! Yes!"

When they finally separated, Autumn was weeping.

"The wedding's back on, I take it?" Teresa said acidly from the staircase.

He took Autumn's hand. "You bet it is, Mrs. Leeds."

"You're sure? I don't think I've ever heard of two people who lied to each other so much in such a short period of time."

Ethan turned back to Autumn, a grin curving the edge of his mouth. "I think I got it all out of my system – how about you, darling?"

"I will never tell another lie as long as I live," Autumn promised.

They kissed again.

"Oh for heaven's sake," Teresa said. "Lily – carry that suitcase back up again. Looks like we'll be staying another day."

Chapter Twenty

June 21st dawned clear and bright as a new penny, as if the sun wanted to make the most of the longest day of the year. For the moment Autumn stood alone on the front porch, but she knew by breakfast time the front lawn would be bustling with workers setting up rows of seats, the latticed archway for the ceremony, and tables for the dinner afterward.

Autumn had been informed by many of Ethan's friends and family that no Western wedding would be complete without a barbeque, so the large roasting pit at the side of the house would soon be in use, its smoke twisting up into the stunning blue sky.

She offered up a prayer of gratitude for everything that had happened since she'd arrived at Chance Creek and the Cruz ranch. Ethan had told her of Lacey's confession and determination to get the help she needed to recover from the abuse she'd received as a young girl. She sent up a prayer for her, too. Now that she wouldn't be around to interfere with Autumn's happiness, she found room in her heart for compassion toward Lacey. No wonder she behaved so spitefully when she'd been treated so badly, herself.

She said a prayer of thanks for her mother and sister's presence at her wedding, too. Teresa already seemed to be coming around to the idea of the marriage and despite her protestations to the contrary, Autumn had a feeling she secretly relished becoming a grandmother. As their mother eased up, Lily relaxed, too – to the point that she had asked whether there were any other cute, unattached cowboys she could dance with at the wedding. Autumn couldn't decide whether to steer her toward Rob, or as far from him as possible. Even Claire had softened up, although maybe that was just Jamie's influence on her.

"Hey, sunshine," Ethan said, coming up behind her and placing a possessive hand on her hip.

"You're not supposed to see me on our wedding day!"

"The sun's not all the way up yet. Think we can sneak in a quickie before the guests arrive?"

Desire stirred within her, as it did whenever Ethan was near. Autumn glanced at her watch. It was still early.

"I think we can get away with it," she said. Taking his hand, she hurried back inside, laughing when he picked her up and headed for the stairs. She exchanged a private look with him at the memory of their lovemaking on the treads beneath their feet as they climbed to the second level of the Big House.

"Shall we go back to bed, or should we try out the linen closet?" he whispered in her ear.

"Linen closet, definitely. The next time I climb into bed with you I want to be your wife."

He enveloped her in a deep kiss. "I love you, Autumn, always and forever."

"I love you always and forever, too."

Cora Seton

About the Author

Cora Seton loves cowboys, country life, gardening, bike-riding, and lazing around with a good book. Mother of four, wife to a computer programmer/eco-farmer, she ditched her California lifestyle eight years ago and moved to a remote logging town in northwestern British Columbia.

Like the characters in her novels, Cora enjoys old-fashioned pursuits and modern technology, spending mornings transforming a neglected one-acre lot into a paradise of orchards, berry bushes and market gardens, and afternoons writing the latest Chance Creek romance novel on her iPad mini. Visit **www.coraseton.com** to read about new releases, locate your favorite characters on the Chance Creek map, and learn about contests and other cool events!

7141367R00136

Printed in Great Britain
by Amazon.co.uk, Ltd.,
Marston Gate.